Jacob wondered what it would be like to be a father.

He led the way to Marissa's car, unable to help but picture several more nights exactly like this one—maybe next time holding hands or bringing her son, Owen, along for a ride on the two-story carousal.

If the kid was anything like his mother, he had to be one amazing little boy.

What would it be like to have a family of his own? Jacob wondered. Marissa was a great mom—that much was obvious in the way her eyes sparkled as she told stories of Owen's antics.

They reached Marissa's SUV, and Jacob paused beside it.

She checked her watch and grimaced. "I better hurry. I told Owen's babysitter I'd be back by nine."

Jacob opened the driver's door for her and grinned. "Mommy to the rescue."

He liked that Owen came first with her. He was liking *a lot* about Marissa.

Books by Betsy St. Amant

Love Inspired

Return to Love
A Valentine's Wish
Rodeo Sweetheart
Mistletoe Prayers
  "Gingerbread Wishes"
Fireman Dad

BETSY ST. AMANT

loves polka-dot shoes, chocolate and sharing the
good news of God's grace through her novels. She
has a bachelor's degree in Christian communications
from Louisiana Baptist University and is actively
pursuing a career in inspirational writing. Betsy
resides in northern Louisiana with her husband
and daughter and enjoys reading, kickboxing and
spending quality time with her family.

Fireman Dad
Betsy St. Amant

Love Inspired

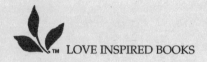

LOVE INSPIRED BOOKS

Recycling programs
for this product may
not exist in your area.

ISBN-13: 978-0-373-81566-1

FIREMAN DAD

Copyright © 2011 by Betsy St. Amant

This edition published by arrangement with Love Inspired Books.

® and TM are trademarks of Love Inspired Books, used under license.
Trademarks indicated with ® are registered in the United States Patent
and Trademark Office, the Canadian Trade Marks Office and in other
countries.

www.LoveInspiredBooks.com

Printed in U.S.A.

I will not leave you nor forsake you.
—*Joshua* 1:5

To my husband, Brandon, for your heart.
You're my everyday hero.

Acknowledgments

Many thanks to my agent, Tamela Hancock Murray,
for your encouragement and for always only
being a phone call away. Also thanks to my editor,
Emily Rodmell, for your excellent editing skills. I have
the best team! Thanks also to my husband, Brandon,
and to Kent Hathorn, for answering those endless,
"would this be believable?" questions
I asked about fire department rank, uniforms,
cars, schedules and everything in betweeen.
And to all firemen everywhere, but especially
in my hometown—thanks for what you do.
You have my full gratitude in a job that rarely sees any.

Chapter One

As usual, Marissa Hawthorne was one knight short of a fairy tale.

She stared at the flat rear tire of her well-used SUV, as if her glare might somehow put more air into the rubber. "Great." Swiping a loose strand of blond hair out of her eyes, she let out a sigh. Just when she thought she'd finally adjusted to widowhood over the years—the empty right side of the bed, the leftovers from dinner, the struggles of single parenting—times like this highlighted the fact that she was truly alone.

Marissa tilted her head and studied the tire. She could probably figure out how to put on the spare, but she doubted her ability to jack up the car by herself. Not to mention the late morning Louisiana humidity had already sent a trail of perspiration down her back, despite the lingering remains of spring. At least she had made it to the parking lot of her event planning office, Your Special Day, before the mangled tire bent the rim and added that expense to the incident. She'd dropped Owen off at school and had turned on Spruce Street to head to work, when she felt the telltale thumping of the wheel.

Marissa braced one arm against the door of the hatch and briefly closed her eyes. Nothing to do but give it her best try—calling her dad was out of the question, nor did she want to shell out extra cash she didn't have to spare for a road service crew.

God, You know I don't ask for a lot of favors anymore. But can't I get a break? Just one? She opened the rear door and tugged at the flooring that covered the spare. Here went nothing.

"Need a hand?"

Marissa jerked upright at the deep voice breaking the silence of the parking lot. A tall, dark-haired man wearing jeans and black sunglasses strolled toward her. She'd been so caught up in her own turmoil she hadn't even heard his truck pull into a space across the lot. Marissa forced a smile, a polite *no* ready to roll off her lips, when the stranger whisked off his sunglasses. Pale blue eyes stared into hers, and her heart stuttered. The stranger's clean-shaven jaw broke into a smile that could have easily thawed winter's chill if the April sun hadn't already long done so. She opened her mouth, but couldn't find her voice.

"I'm Jacob Greene." He held out his hand and she shook it, mentally kicking herself for the distraction. *He's only a man, Marissa, not a celebrity.* Although he certainly could have been, with those chiseled good looks. In fact, he almost seemed familiar—but she couldn't place how.

She cleared her throat. "Marissa Hawthorne. I own Your Special Day." She released his hand and pointed to the store behind them.

"Then you're the lady I was coming to see." He smiled again, his teeth white and even against his tanned skin. His gaze drifted to her SUV. "And it looks like I was just in time."

You have no idea. Maybe God was still in the business of answering her prayers after all. Marissa smiled back. "I hate to play the damsel in distress, but I have to admit, this one has me stumped. I'd say I was having a Monday, if this wasn't Wednesday."

Jacob laughed. "I know what you mean. We all have those days." He easily removed the tire from the hatch and set it on the ground. "I can have you ready to go in a few minutes."

"I really appreciate it. It's not a big rush, since I'm already at work. I just need to be able to pick up my son later this afternoon from school." She pushed up the sleeves of her thin, peasant-style blouse, trying to force her eyes away from the tight lines of muscle in Jacob's arms as he worked the lug nuts loose on the flat.

Jacob's eyes darted to hers, then back to the tire as he worked. "That shouldn't be an issue. How old is your son?"

"Owen's seven." Marissa tugged absently at the necklace she wore every day—an amethyst symbolizing Owen's February birthday—her stomach churning at the realization of how quickly her baby boy was growing up. Time was flying fast—too fast. Kevin had been dead almost five years now, and she'd been back in her hometown of Orchid Hill, Louisiana, for a little over a year. Sometimes it seemed as if the last few years were nothing but a dream.

Sometimes a nightmare.

"I have a niece who is about to turn seven." Jacob wrestled the jack into place and began to hike up the SUV. He grunted with the effort. "She goes to Orchid Hill Elementary."

"So does Owen."

Jacob grinned. "Small world."

"I'm not sure about that, but it's definitely a small town." Marissa looked away, her fingers zipping over the necklace chain as she pretended to study something over her shoulder. Did he have any idea the effect of those dimples? They were downright dangerous.

She shouldn't notice such things. Dating was not a priority—Owen remained planted at the top of that short list, which meant work lingered a close second in order to provide for her son. Thankfully business had been good. At least the recession didn't seem to stop people from celebrating the milestones in their lives.

A familiar tsunami of regret washed over Marissa, mingling with the wind that teased the loose hairs from her hastily applied clip. Happy as she was with Owen, Marissa couldn't help the melancholy that sometimes took over when she was planning a wedding shower or anniversary party for a client. She and Kevin might not have had the happiest of marriages, and he might have put his firefighting career over his family to a fault—just like her father—but it was still hard to face the fact that she would likely never get to celebrate an anniversary again. As a single mom and a business owner, who had time for anything else?

She tore her gaze away from the navy T-shirt stretching across Jacob's broad shoulders. Nope, no point in noticing his dimples. Or his muscles. Or the way his dark hair curled over his forehead—

Marissa jerked as the wrench clattered to the pavement. Jacob removed the flat tire and began to assemble the spare. "Be sure not to drive on this thing for very long—or very fast. The last thing you want is a blowout."

"No kidding." Marissa shuddered. "Thank you again for your help. I'd have been stuck." If not physically stuck, then financially—or emotionally if she'd been forced to cave and call her dad to bail her out.

Jacob tightened the last of the lug nuts and stood, swiping his hands on the legs of his pants before placing the tools and the flat back into the hatch. "Think nothing of it. I'm glad to help a— what'd you call yourself? Damsel in distress?" He grinned, then shut the rear door and wiped sweat from his forehead with his shirtsleeve.

Marissa's business skills snapped back into effect at his tired gesture, and she motioned toward her office. "Come on inside, let me get you some water. It's the least I can do."

"That sounds good." Jacob fell into step beside her as they crossed the lot to her small, but functional, office space. He opened the door for her. "Ladies first."

Apparently chivalry wasn't dead in Orchid Hill, after all. Marissa thanked him and hurried to grab a bottle of water from the dorm fridge she kept beside her desk. She handed it to him. "Have a seat."

"Nice place." Jacob twisted the lid off the bottle and took a long sip as he looked around the open room, painted yellow with a mural of balloons and children on the far wall, and she couldn't help but warm at the compliment. He paused to touch the top of a bobble-head clown on the bookshelf that held party theme books. "Festive. Olivia would love that."

"Olivia?" His girlfriend, probably. Good thing she decided to put thoughts of his dimples far away. Marissa sat down behind her desk, grateful to be back on her own turf. She might not know anything about changing tires, but she knew party planning. Maybe she could offer Jacob—and Olivia—a discount for his help.

"Olivia is my niece." Jacob took the chair across from her desk and finished his water with a quick swig.

Niece. Not girlfriend. Marissa tried to ignore the relief that seeped into her stomach and nodded for him to go on.

"That's why I came to your store in the first place, actually," Jacob continued.

"So it wasn't because you received my desperate SOS signal?" Marissa grinned, then regretted the way her heart thumped when Jacob smiled back, dimples on high alert.

"I thought I heard something." He laughed. "Seriously, though, I was hoping to hire you to plan my niece's birthday party."

"Sounds good." Marissa flipped open her leather

day planner and fanned through the pages. Hopefully he wouldn't choose the weeks coming up that she had blocked off for the upcoming fundraiser. A city budget cut had recently led to a decision to lay off six firemen, and members of Orchid Hill Church asked Marissa to organize a big fundraiser for the affected families. As the daughter of one fireman and the widow of another, Marissa could relate all too easily to the families involved and was glad someone had come up with a way to help.

Even if her father, Fire Chief Lyle Brady, wasn't nearly as thrilled by Marissa's participation.

Marissa tapped her calendar with her pen. "What date did you have in mind?"

Jacob offered a sheepish shrug. "That's where my next question comes in. It's sort of short notice."

Marissa looked up. "How short?"

"Less than three weeks away."

"How much less?" Marissa's eyebrows rose.

Jacob's lips twisted to the side. "Four days?"

She couldn't help but laugh. "The party is supposed to be in two weeks and three days?"

"Hey, you're quick with math." He winked, and her stomach flipped with regret at the thought of disappointing him. She had a policy about last-minute parties—she didn't take them. But how could she turn him down when he had just done her a huge favor with her car?

She drew a deep breath. It was business, nothing personal. Surely he would understand. "I wish I could, but I have a policy against short notices. It takes time away from Owen." She gestured to the framed photo on her cherry credenza, where Owen struck a muscle-man pose for the camera. Feeling wistful, she admired his silky blond hair that matched her own. "Being a single mom is rough enough without working overtime." That was the understatement of the century.

"I'm sure it does."

Why Marissa wanted to share more with him, she didn't know. She swallowed. "I'm a widow."

Jacob's sky blue eyes met hers, full of compassion and something else she couldn't identify. Respect? Admiration? "I'm sorry to hear that."

Marissa lifted one shoulder in a shrug and forced a small smile. "It all happened a long time ago." More like a lifetime.

Jacob nodded slowly. "Listen, Marissa. Normally I would accept your reasons and leave it at that, but I'm sort of desperate. I want my niece to have the celebration she deserves." His expression tightened. "Olivia's family has had a rough couple of weeks, and their budget is tight, to put it mildly. I don't want that to affect her birthday. They've all been through enough."

Marissa's resolve weakened. Handsome, charming *and* a family man. She shouldn't be following that train of thought, but it chugged into her head regardless as she stared at her day planner. Maybe she could squeeze in one birthday party for a deserving little girl—but no, she didn't even have a location nailed down yet for the fundraiser. If she overbooked herself now, that event would suffer, and the families of the firemen would be even more disappointed than they already were.

She clicked her ballpoint pen on and off, debating, then slowly shook her head. "I admire that and wish I could make an exception. I really do—but a big festival has my schedule tighter than usual right now."

"What festival is that?" Jacob leaned forward as if truly interested in what Marissa had to say. When was the last time a man had looked at her in that way?

She shook her head to clear it. "The Fireman's Festival—to raise money for the families of the local firemen who were recently laid off."

Jacob's eyes widened. "You're the woman organizing the fundraiser? My church is the one that hired you." He smiled. "Like I said, small world."

No kidding. If she knew guys like Jacob still went to church, she might have given it another try instead of spending Sundays sleeping in with Owen. Her faith took a hit after Kevin's death, and so far church brought more grief than healing. It was easier to drown reality in iced Pop-Tarts and cartoons while snuggling with her little man.

Marissa forced her thoughts back to the present. "How'd you hear about Your Special Day if not through your church?"

"Newspaper advertisement."

Good to know that chunk of money had been a good investment. Though, at this point, a partially wasted one, since she wouldn't be able to plan the birthday party for him and his niece.

Jacob hooked one ankle over the other, as if settling in for a long conversation. "I know the church appreciates your taking the job. Pastor Rob mentioned the generous discount you're paying forward to the cause."

A warm flush crept up Marissa's neck. She'd hoped to keep that part quiet—it was embarrassing, especially if people found out how emotionally against the profession of firefighting she remained in the first place. No one would understand why she was doing it. But then again, most people weren't twenty-eight-year-old widows of a fireman, struggling to raise a child alone. "It's not a big deal. Not compared to what these guys are going through, I'm sure."

Though, a part of her couldn't help but think the laid-off firemen's wives had to be relieved. After the uniformed men lowered Kevin's casket into the ground, Marissa held Owen close and promised herself that if she ever dated again, any future prospects would have a desk job—something safe, with predictable hours and lots of free time for family. Between her late husband and her father, she was through with missed holidays and shift work. She wanted to be number one in someone's life.

That is, if she ever figured out how to live again.

The first thing Jacob Greene had noticed when he had walked across the parking lot was the beautiful, petite blonde wrestling with the hatch floorboard of her SUV. After she'd mentioned her son, his heart sank. Of course someone like her would have been snatched up long ago. But the mention of her single status and that telltale bare ring finger lifted his spirits a second time.

Jacob smiled at Marissa from across her office desk. The water he'd chugged down churned in his stomach at her sweet grin of response. He hoped he hadn't made too big an idiot of himself, staring at her the way he had outside when he first arrived. He'd been tempted to leave the sunglasses on to prevent her from noticing during his stroll across the lot. But she'd finally introduced herself in that confident, slightly Southern voice that warmed his insides like his favorite cinnamon rolls and settled in just as sweet, and he couldn't help but relax.

And speaking of sweet—it took a special woman to get involved with a fundraiser like she was doing, for people she likely didn't even know. Beautiful *and* compassionate. He hadn't found that combination in a long time—and he'd certainly been looking.

With a start, Jacob realized he was staring again, but so was Marissa. He knew he should say something more to persuade her to plan his niece's party—especially considering if a small business such as Your Special Day couldn't find time to do him a favor, the larger companies in town were probably booked solid, too. But he was afraid that the moment he opened his mouth he'd mention something about how that flowered top brought out her green eyes, and he'd be in big trouble.

Marissa cleared her throat and broke the connection between them. "Again, I'm sorry. I wish there was time."

Jacob hesitated. He hated being pushy, but he couldn't bear the disappointment on Olivia's face—or his sister-in-law's—if he came home proverbially empty-handed. His brother's wife, Liz, would insist it didn't matter—but he said he'd do this for them, and he wanted to keep his word. Anyone could throw together a bunch of Mylar balloons and sprinkle confetti on a table. He wanted Olivia's party to be done right. If their financial situation hadn't changed, Liz would have gone all out for her only daughter, and he intended to do the same.

Hence his desperation for Marissa to take the job. Jacob could have just handed Liz the cash and told her to get whatever she wanted for the party, but she had enough on her plate. She deserved the break and the chance to be involved with Olivia on her big day instead of stuck in the kitchen cutting cake and cleaning up messes like in years past. He needed Marissa to say yes.

Jacob clicked his tongue, stalling. "Maybe I could help you out somehow with the fundraiser, so you're not so swamped. Then you could do both."

Marissa raised one eyebrow, and he took that as a sign that she was considering his random proposition. He rushed on before she lost interest. "I own a lawn business. I could help with ground prep or flower planting for the fundraiser. Whatever you needed—on one condition, of course." He grinned, and Marissa smiled back before she glanced down at her planner.

Hopefully they could strike a deal and both get something they needed. Besides, it was the least he could do to volunteer his side job services, after his brother's job was cut at the station and not his own. Jacob had more seniority within the fire department, having worked three years longer than Ryan had, but he'd been the one to convince his little brother to go for it in the first place. Ryan had aced the academy and dedicated himself to two years of service, and what had it gotten him? A tiny severance and a big goodbye.

"That's nice of you to offer." Marissa looked up. "But I don't even have a confirmed location yet. We can't use your church because of weddings that are booked there the entire month of May. This is a busy time of year."

He could fix that, too. "Hey, I have ten acres south of the city limits. That should be plenty of room for whatever you have plànned." He gave a pointed look to the blank pages in front of her. "Or *will* have planned."

She laughed. "It is sort of hard to make arrangements when you aren't sure of the venue." Marissa rolled in her lower lip and she studied him in some sort of unofficial test. He met her gaze full-on, and tried to ignore the attraction flickering in his stomach. *Business, this is business.* Even if she was one of the most beautiful women he'd come across in a long time.

Marissa inhaled. "One condition, huh?"

"Two guesses what it might be." He winked.

Her mouth twitched into a smile, and Jacob fought to keep his own in check. He must have passed her scrutiny, because she finally nodded. "I'll have to see the property for myself before I can say for sure, but I think I will take you up on that offer. One last-minute party for ten acres of fundraising." She held out her hand.

"It's a deal." Jacob shook her hand for the second time that day, trying not to dwell on how soft her palm felt against his calloused one. "You won't regret it." Not to mention having the festival on his own property would make the landscaping aspect easier, since he kept his yard up regularly. He'd never been a fan of the guys in the department who ran side businesses like his and didn't even maintain their own yards. What would a client think if they drove by his house and saw knee-high weeds?

"I really appreciate this." Marissa settled back into her chair, crossing one leg over the other and relaxing as if a burden had been lifted.

"What, being coerced?" Jacob laughed. "Happy to help."

She chuckled. "Now that I have a location, I can get started on the fun stuff."

"Which is?" he prodded, wanting her to keep smiling.

"The *when* and *where* are important," she answered. "But the *what*—that's the good part."

She was cute when she was in her element. Jacob crossed his arms over his chest, his turn to study her now. "So *what* is your vision for the fundraiser?"

"I was originally hoping to pull off a mini-car-

nival, but was afraid I wouldn't have the space."
She gestured at him. "But I think ten acres will
suffice."

"Well, it's technically about nine. I do have a
house on part of it." He winced in mock dread.
"Is that a deal breaker?"

A flirty spark lit Marissa's eyes, and she held
up one finger in a warning. "We already shook on
it, so don't think you can back out that easily."

Her teasing gaze linked with his, and a rush of
warmth filled Jacob's chest. "Trust me. Backing
out is not on the agenda."

Chapter Two

❧

Marissa inched her SUV forward in the line of cars, all waiting for Orchid Hill Elementary to open its doors and release a horde of children from its red-bricked depths. She kept one eye out for Owen, grateful the crossing guard was on duty in his bright yellow vest and hat. Owen was usually a pretty cautious child, but sometimes his excitement ran away with him and made him less than careful.

He was like his father that way.

Her cell rang and Marissa dug it out of her purse. "Hello?" She craned her head to see around the car in front of her. Owen must still be waiting with his teacher in the school yard.

"Marissa, hi. This is Jacob Greene."

She was glad her foot was already on the brake, or she'd have jerked her SUV to a dead halt. "Oh! Hi. Hello." The words filtered out more like a croak than a greeting, and she mentally chided herself for the lack of professionalism.

He hesitated. "Did I catch you at a bad time?"

"No, I'm just picking up Owen from school." She cleared her throat, hoping to eliminate the frog that seemed to have taken up residence. When she gave Jacob her business card yesterday at the office, she never imagined he'd have called so soon—or at all, for that matter.

"Gotcha." He laughed. "I've picked up Olivia before—I know that can be a rough crowd."

"No kidding."

Jacob continued. "Were you able to get that tire fixed?"

"Yes, after work yesterday. There was a nail, so they patched it. I'm good to go, thanks to you."

"Nah, I didn't do much. Nothing anyone else wouldn't have done." Jacob brushed off the compliment, and Marissa couldn't help but admire the humility. Kevin had always soaked in—even sought out—praise, always trying to be the hero. But why was she comparing them?

She licked her dry lips. "So, what's up? Did you have another idea for your niece's party?" Surely he hadn't called only to check on her tire.

"Actually, I was calling to ask you a question." Now it was Jacob's turn to clear his throat, and Marissa could have sworn she detected a hint of apprehension beneath the cough. "Do you have plans for Friday evening?"

She never had plans on a Friday night, unless you counted the occasional pizza-and-a-movie outing with Owen, or the weekends she spent with her laptop catching up on work. "Not at the moment." She wanted to ask why, but held her tongue, afraid to hope. He wasn't asking her out. They'd just met yesterday and he was hiring her as a professional event planner. *Come back to real life, Marissa. This isn't one of Owen's Disney DVDs.*

"I was wondering if you'd like to meet me at the Boardwalk downtown."

Her cell phone slipped from her fingers into her lap. Marissa scrambled to grab it as the woman in the van behind her honked the horn. "The Boardwalk?" She accelerated into the vacated spot ahead in line, her thoughts racing even faster. The Orchid Hill Boardwalk was a huge shopping district on the river outside of downtown, with a movie theater, restaurants and a giant two-story carousal. It was considered to be a popular dating scene among couples of all ages, though family-oriented as well. She'd taken Owen a few Saturdays ago for an ice cream cone and new shoes. But going with Jacob on a Friday night—that was different. She'd need to find a babysitter, and something to wear, and—

"They have several party goods stores and a garden nursery, so I thought we could get a head start on the birthday party plans and what you might need for the fundraiser."

Marissa jerked back to the present as reality crashed around her. Her heart thumped an unsteady rhythm and she gripped the steering wheel tighter with her free hand. Not a date. She ignored the rock of disappointment in her stomach. Probably for the best—business, she was used to. Dating, not so much.

Jacob's voice rose slightly in volume. "Hello? Are you still there?"

She realized with a start she hadn't answered. "Yes, sorry. Just...driving." More like driving herself crazy. She briefly closed her eyes to straighten her shaky world back on its axis.

"Is that a yes to my invitation, or a yes that you're still there?" Jacob's teasing tone warmed her more than the sun reflecting off the dashboard and onto her bare forearms, and the disappointment faded slightly.

Marissa smiled. "Both." Why not? Might as well discuss business outside on the Boardwalk instead of at her desk, where she stayed cooped up most days. She hadn't been out with anyone other than Owen or her mother in a long time.

Too long.

"Great." Jacob let out an exhale. "If you give me your address, I'd be happy to pick you up."

"Thanks, but I'll just meet you there." Of course Jacob would be a gentleman and want to pick her up, even for a business meeting, but she had one hard-and-fast rule—Owen didn't meet any men in her life until it had the potential to be serious. If this wasn't even a date, then there was no need to confuse—or egg on—her son. Owen had been trying to convince Marissa to go on dates for months.

"No problem. I'll see you at the Boardwalk at six-thirty, then."

"See you then." Marissa said goodbye and hung up, relieved Jacob hadn't pushed the issue of meeting him. She would hate to make things awkward by explaining her reasons, but when it came to Owen, his welfare came first—even if that decision often had her keeping people at arm's length.

Marissa peered around the car in front of her and finally spotted Owen jogging toward the SUV. She unlocked the back passenger door and he climbed inside, shrugging off his backpack and tossing it on the seat beside him. "Hey, buddy, how was your day?" Could he tell how flushed she felt? She aimed the AC vent toward her neck and turned to her son with a smile, trying to push aside the remaining disappointment lingering in her stomach. If Jacob had asked her on a real date, would she have even said yes? But it didn't matter. There was no use analyzing what hadn't happened.

Owen reached for his seat belt with a grin. "School was super cool!"

His hair was rumpled and he smelled like he'd had a little too much fun at recess, but that didn't stop Marissa from stretching toward him. "Where's my kiss?"

Owen rolled his eyes, but leaned forward and allowed a quick kiss on his forehead before he buckled in. Marissa fastened her own belt and merged into traffic. "What was the super cool part?" With Owen, that could be anything from finding a frog at recess to getting a decent grade on a math quiz. Either would be equally shocking. At least he made up for his lack of math ability with excellent reading and writing skills.

"Firemen came to our school today!"

Marissa's eyes darted to the rearview mirror. Her own shock stared back in the reflection. Owen bounced in his seat, his eyes lit with excitement. "They talked about safety and stuff. We should check the batteries in our smoke detectors. Have you checked them?" He bounced again. "Have you?"

Marissa's hands clenched around the steering wheel and she worked to keep her voice even. "Yes, buddy, I did a few weeks ago." How could his class have done a fire safety demonstration without a notice? The teacher should have sent something out to the parents—though most parents wouldn't have the same issues with it that she did. Her knuckles whitened. If her father had arranged for this and didn't even bother to tell her—

"One of the firemen pulled a quarter from my ear and he let me keep it!" Owen held up a shiny coin and flipped it from one palm to the other. "See? He was so cool! He told me all about firefighting and how I could do it one day, too, if I wanted. Like Grandpa and Daddy."

Marissa forced a smile in the mirror at Owen as she flipped on the blinker. "That is pretty exciting." Only halfway listening as he rattled on about fire trucks and all the equipment the firefighters had shown him, Marissa made a sharp left and veered off course toward Oak Street.

She had a stop to make.

"Grandpa!" Owen ran inside Central Station ahead of Marissa into his grandfather's office.

Fire Chief Lyle Brady twisted in his leather swivel chair, eyes widening with a flicker of surprise. "Well, this is a shock. What brings you two by?"

Marissa leaned against the doorjamb as her dad opened his arms to Owen. Owen hesitated, then edged toward him with a shy grin—which

promptly faded upon inspection of his grandfather's desk. All evidence of shyness erased,
Owen tilted his head to one side. "Hey, where's
the candy? You used to have caramel squares on
your desk."

Marissa bit back a snort. There was the son she
knew and loved.

"The receptionist has it at her desk now." Chief
patted his ample stomach. "It was too tempting at
close range."

"Can I have a piece?" Owen asked his grandpa,
then caught himself and met Marissa's gaze instead. "I mean, may I have a piece, Mom?"

"Sure, buddy. You go get some candy and let me
talk to Grandpa alone for a minute." She stepped
sideways as Owen barreled past to charm the receptionist out of her candy bowl.

"That doesn't sound good." Chief crossed his
arms over his chest. "But you haven't been by in
months, so I'm not surprised there's some kind of
reason now."

"The door opens both ways, Dad." Marissa
folded her arms in front of her racing heart, mirroring her father's image.

"Is this about the fundraiser and the layoffs?"
His thick eyebrows furrowed nearly into one. "I
told you it's not good politics for family to be involved in business. This thing could get messy."

Marissa inhaled, intending to count to ten but

only getting to four. "Trust me, you've made your stand on that clear. But that's not why I came."

"Go on." He leaned forward.

Marissa bit her lip, fighting the swirl of emotions raging in her stomach. She waited until the boiling cauldron settled. "I can't believe you arranged for your men to speak to Owen's class at school and didn't at least warn me."

"Warn you? Is that all?" Her father laughed, a booming, husky sound she never heard often enough growing up. He relaxed backward, his bulk causing the chair to squeak. "They were telling the kids to stay away from matches, not escorting them through a live drill."

"It was more than that, and you know it." Marissa's voice rose against her will and she quickly glanced over her shoulder down the hall into the lobby. Owen was attempting to juggle three caramel squares as he told the receptionist about his homework assignment. Just in case, Marissa stepped inside the office and shut the door behind her all but a crack.

Her father's eyebrows rose, but to his credit he waited for her to finish.

"All Owen talked about the entire drive here was how cool the firemen were and how he wants to drive a fire truck when he grows up." She bit back the rest of Owen's sentence before the words could leave her mouth. *Just like Grandpa.*

She swallowed. *Just like Daddy.*

He shrugged. "Hey, firemen *are* pretty cool."

"Dad." Marissa's eyes narrowed. Would he ever take her seriously? Did he not care that she lost her family because of the career he held in such high esteem?

Chief Brady released a heavy sigh and braced his elbows against the desk. "Marissa, you're overreacting." Creases marred the skin by his eyes, more so than she remembered noticing the last time she'd seen him. But that had been like he said—months ago. In fact, probably not since Owen's school play around President's Day. Even though she'd been back in Orchid Hill for some time now, her father remained absent as usual. Her mom made efforts to stop by at least once a week with treats for Owen, but the chief rarely came along, choosing to spend his time at the office instead.

Not that she minded all that much. Over the years, Marissa and her father had reached some kind of silent agreement to disagree, about—well, everything. Sometimes the absence made it easier.

Even if it did still rub her heart raw.

Her dad continued, "Owen is seven, not seventeen. He's going to want to be a cowboy, an astronaut and a pro ball player over the next couple of years. Take it with a grain of salt." He shrugged. "He's a boy. Boys have big dreams."

"But we don't have anyone in our family who flies into space or rides rodeos for a living." Marissa shot a pointed glance at the framed certificates, awards and degrees decorating the office walls. "Your career is already an influence on him." A fact that kept her up more nights than she liked to admit, locked in fear of the future because of the past. Maybe Kevin's death was chalked up to an accident, but accidents happened in the world of firefighting.

A lot.

Her dad flexed his hands, popping his knuckles. "It's a career I happen to love, Marissa."

No kidding. The bitterness felt heavy on her tongue and Marissa swallowed, looking away as emotion burned in her throat. She wouldn't get into the past here, not now. It wouldn't matter anyway—she'd learned that tear-filled lesson years ago. With her Dad, work always came first.

Apparently it still did.

"I can't promise to go out of my way to steer Owen in an opposite direction." Chief Brady shrugged, one broad shoulder straining against the neck of his white uniform. "I'm sorry, but if he wants to be a fireman one day, there are worse careers to have."

"There are also much safer ones."

Chief tapped his fingers against his desktop, a tick that meant he'd reached a new level of frustration and was trying to hold it back. She might not have learned the sound of his laughter over the years, but she'd certainly learned his tells of anger. He released a sigh. "Marissa, there's enough stress around this office right now with the layoffs and negative publicity from the press. This isn't a big deal, and I beg you not to make it one."

Marissa lowered her voice until it whispered through her lips. "In case you forgot, Owen doesn't have a dad and I don't have a husband because of your *beloved* career."

Chief didn't meet her eyes, but the tapping increased as he stared at his desk calendar. A flicker of guilt made Marissa wonder if she'd gone too far, but she pushed it aside. It was impossible to go too far with Chief. He was never around to notice. He might have climbed the ranks in the department faster than most men his age, but at what cost? His desk, organized and neat like his dresser and nightstand had always been at home, lay void of anything personal or resembling family. No photos. No mementos.

No, some things never changed at all.

Marissa drew a steadying breath. "Listen, I don't expect you to understand. I just expect you to treat me with the respect I deserve as a mother—and *not* warning me about your men doing a presentation for Owen's class feels disrespectful. Not to mention that one of your men crossed the line by turning a safety presentation into a personal recruiting session. I should have a say in who and what influences my child."

"It's the teacher's job to notify parents about school demonstrations, not the department's."

"But you're my father."

He flinched, a movement so fast Marissa wondered if she'd imagined it. "Forget it. I shouldn't have come." She turned to the door and wrenched it open.

Chief coughed. "If it makes you happy, I'll make sure you're aware of any future presentations. Okay?"

Her back turned, Marissa nodded with little conviction. It was as much of an olive branch as her dad could offer right now.

And as much of one as she was willing to take.

Marissa plastered on a smile as she started down the hallway, stepping back into the comfortable, if not slightly worn, shoes of her role as Mommy. "Come on, Owen! Time to go home."

They were done here.

Jacob kicked his booted feet up on the coffee table, glad this wasn't his night to cook at the station. They'd just gotten back from working a wreck involving an eighteen-wheeler, a flipped car and one severely dented guardrail. Two hours in the relentless sun doing hazardous material checks and getting the truck driver transported from mangled cab to gurney proved exhausting. Thankfully the driver of the car was all right and had gone to the E.R. as a precaution. Some nights, that wasn't the case.

Some nights, Jacob possessed no appetite for dinner at all.

"Jacob, Captain said he heard there's a chance to catch an overtime shift tomorrow. You interested?" Steve Mitchell, driver for their station, hollered from the kitchen, around the corner from where Jacob sat.

"If they hadn't let six men go, they wouldn't have an overtime shift to fill." Regret coated Jacob's tongue and he bit back any more negative comments. As much as he struggled to keep business and family separate, the city council was making it tricky. If Jacob wasn't offended by their actions, then he felt guilty of not being a good brother. But if he clung to the guilt, then he grew afraid his work ethic would crash or his bitterness would be revealed to the chiefs—and then his own job would be at risk if there were more layoffs. But that train of thought carried him full circle back to a new guilt of caring for his own welfare when his brother's was tossed aside.

He was getting sick of no-win situations.

"Couldn't hear you." Steve popped his head around the corner, wiping his hands on a dish towel. Whatever he was cooking already smelled burnt, and Jacob's stomach protested with disappointment. If he had the energy, he would've taken over with the wooden spoon, but not tonight.

Jacob tugged the leg of his pants further down over his boot. "Just think it's strange they're offering overtime right now."

"Well, they do have a sudden lack of manpower." Steve disappeared back into the kitchen.

"Exactly." It wasn't the first time Jacob had questioned the political aspects of the department—though it was likely for the best not to know all the details. Maybe once his brother found a new job, Jacob could relax and work would once again be like it used to be. He raised his voice so Steve could hear above the hum of the oven range vent. "Count me out. If you want to sign up for the shift, go ahead."

Steve's head poked around the frame a second time, reminding Jacob of a prairie dog. "That's weird. You used to always jump at overtime offers. What's changed?"

"Nothing." Nothing other than his meeting with Marissa tomorrow, that is. But that was none of Steve's business, and if Steve knew, he'd definitely take it out of context. Jacob had his fill of department gossip a few months ago when a woman he took out *one* time decided to pop in the station the next day with two dozen brownies. Needless to say, she hadn't taken his gentle rejection very well. He shuddered at the memory.

"There's got to be something," Steve persisted. "Another hot date?" The food on the stove splattered and hissed behind him, and he darted back into the kitchen. "Make sure this one brings brownies again." He laughed.

"No date. Business." But even though Jacob said they'd discuss the fundraiser and the birthday party for Olivia, more and more it seemed the only thing he really wanted to discuss was Marissa Hawthorne. Who was she? What did she like? What did she do in her free time? Something about her smile seemed infectious, and business or not, he was looking forward to tomorrow night probably more than he should.

Steve let out an exaggerated sigh from the kitchen. "Surprise, surprise. You never date—with the exception of the brownie girl."

"Her name was Lisa."

"You should have taken her out again. She could cook."

It figured Steve found that one particular quality alone worthy of a long-time commitment. Jacob snorted and grabbed a motorcycle magazine from the coffee table. "Why don't you worry more about our food in there and less about my love life, huh?" He flipped through the glossy pages. More like lack of love life. It was true he hadn't dated a lot lately. To his regret, the last few women he'd taken out were like Lisa—overeager, clingy and more interested in the physical than getting to know one another. He might be a red-blooded male, but his faith came first. Besides, they hadn't connected. It was simple—either the spark was there, or it wasn't.

With Marissa, there were so many sparks his palm felt like the Fourth of July when they shook hands.

He turned another page. Not that it mattered. They were going to be planning a fundraiser together, so her beauty didn't count in that respect. So what if she was sweet? He smiled. And funny. And had eyes that seemed to reach clear—

The smoke detector in the kitchen blared at the same time as the overhead distress alarms. *Time to go.* Jacob jumped up and tossed the magazine on the table, glad he'd left his boots on. Steve moaned from the kitchen as a lid slammed against a pot. "Figures! Right when dinner is almost ready."

Captain Walker brushed past them toward the bay, snorting as he headed for the trucks. "We've had enough soot and ash today already, Steve. It'll keep."

"It wasn't looking *that* bad." Steve grabbed the broom they kept in the pantry and jabbed the smoke detector on the ceiling. The piercing shriek stopped, but the fire alarms continued to sound.

"Engine four, trauma four. Fire reported at 6500 Dudley Square. Flames and smoke visible." The dispatcher's tone echoed through the small living area. "First party report. All units advise."

"House fire." Adrenaline rushed through Jacob's chest, overflowing his senses with the familiar combination of anxiety and excitement. He followed Captain into the bay, the scent of exhaust fumes and disinfectant assaulting his nostrils. He hoped this house wouldn't be a goner like the last one his shift had worked a few weeks back. As often as he saw the destruction left behind by a fire's greedy pulse, the sight of ruined memories and heirlooms never failed to burn something deep inside him. Jacob grabbed his bunker gear from the hooks on the wall and shrugged his arms into the sleeves before swinging up inside the backseat of the cab.

Steve took the driver's seat and cranked the engine, his earlier joking set aside as professionalism took over. Captain buckled his seat belt as Steve flipped on the sirens. "Here we go."

Jacob tugged on his Nomex hood, then grabbed the overhead bar as they squealed onto the street, lights flashing. He peered out the window as they accelerated around the curve. Man, he loved his job. Despite the politics, firefighting ran in his

blood. Around him, the world continued to revolve as usual—drivers heading to various des-
tinations, pedestrians strolling the sidewalks and
enjoying the warm spring air and the aroma of
flowers blooming on the landscaped street corners. But a few blocks away, someone's world had
gotten yanked off center.

And with God's help, he would help make it
right again.

Chapter Three

Thick clouds threatened to block the warm evening sun as Marissa exited the parking garage and strolled across the imitation cobblestoned street of the Boardwalk. Her high heel wobbled once, and she suddenly wished she'd worn flip-flops and jeans. Owen had been the one to choose the silky red top she paired with black dress pants—probably because he'd been racing his equally red fire truck around her closet floor at the time. Was the look too professional for the Boardwalk? The shade of red too loud for a date?

Not date—business outing, she corrected. In which case color shouldn't matter. Too late now, anyway. She was already five minutes late after dropping Owen off at her neighbor's.

Marissa paused by a cotton candy vendor and scanned the open pavilion of shops for Jacob, willing the nerves in her stomach to settle. Although she often met clients outside the office to discuss party plans, it was usually at their homes or for a casual lunch. Never had she met a single, attractive male—in the evening. Alone. Did it give the wrong impression?

A mild breeze cooled the perspiration on the back of Marissa's neck and fluttered the hem of a child's sundress as she ran past Marissa, clutching a tall cone of cotton candy. A teenage couple ambled by, holding hands, and a handsome man in a pale blue dress shirt leaned against the railing overlooking the colored water fountain a few yards to her left. He turned as if he felt Marissa's scrutiny, and raised his arm with a smile.

Jacob. Marissa's breath caught and she clutched the thin strap of her purse. He looked different than he had the other day, more distinguished— yet still borderline familiar somehow. Dark hair, almost touching his collar, set off his tanned, healthy complexion, and a hint of five o'clock stubble dotted his jaw. He'd been clean-shaven last time she saw him.

She couldn't decide which look made him more handsome.

At least he'd dressed up a little, too, which eased her apprehension about her own attire. Marissa made her way toward Jacob, hoping her smile revealed professionalism and not lingering nerves. She really should get out more if a mere business meeting set her off like this.

"Hey, there." Jacob's gaze, seemingly electric against the blue of his shirt, drew her in as she joined him at the railing. A myriad of colored water sprayed cheerily into the air before them. If she didn't know better, she would have found the setting more than a little romantic.

"Hi. Sorry I'm a little late. Owen couldn't decide what he wanted to bring with him to the babysitter's." Marissa braced her weight against the railing. "I had to talk him out of taking every toy he owns."

Jacob grinned. "If Owen is anything like my niece, I'd guess that wasn't the first time you've had that conversation."

"You'd guess right." Marissa relaxed under his appreciative gaze. "My mom usually comes over to watch Owen on the rare occasions I need to go out, but she wasn't available tonight. Nanas tend to have more patience with that sort of thing."

"I know my parents spoil Olivia rotten. But she's a good enough kid not to let it go to her head." Jacob gestured to the row of shops to their right. "Shall we start with the plant nursery?"

"Sounds good." Marissa's spine tingled at the light pressure of Jacob's guiding hand as they turned toward the garden store. She'd been around attractive men before, but something about Jacob felt different. Unnerving, and a little foreign—in a good way.

Maybe too good. He was, after all, her new client.

They walked side by side past the storefronts. Jacob paused in front of a toy store window and grinned. "I've always found it funny how kids seem to instantly know which family member they can wrap around their finger the tightest. With Olivia, that person is definitely her papa— my dad. Of course, he never minds."

Marissa turned her lips up in a smile, but the motion felt forced. Hopefully Jacob wouldn't notice. This wasn't the time to get into a conversation about Owen's lack of relationship with his own grandfather. But she couldn't help the melancholy ache that spread across her chest. Memories of their argument from yesterday clouded her previously good mood. She pretended to study the collection of dolls on display until the heavy moment passed.

"You okay?" Jacob turned away from the window toward her, concern etched in his expression.

Marissa tried to brighten the plastic smile as they started walking again. "I'm fine. It's that… Owen isn't close to his grandparents. My mom, somewhat, but not my dad." She swallowed the lump in her throat. "Which is partly my fault. I'm not close with my dad, either." She looked away, sudden heat flooding her neck. *Great, Marissa, why don't you just plop your family issues right here on the cobblestones in front of him?*

"I'm sorry to hear that." Jacob hesitated before pulling open the door of the nursery. "Would you like to talk about it?"

Marissa shook her head abruptly. "No. Thanks, though. It's not a big deal. I'd rather talk about the fundraiser."

"If you're sure." Concern lingered in his expression as he pulled open the door.

It was sweet of him to care. But this wasn't the time—and with him as her client, there would never be the right time. It simply wasn't his business.

Even if the sympathy in his eyes made her want to spill the whole story.

Marissa took a deep breath and allowed the air-conditioning rushing through the open doorway to cool her flushed face. "Maybe this place will give us some ideas for what we'll need to finish the festival. I'd really like to find a way to include the kids that attend."

"This nursery is one of the best." Jacob pointed to a row of plants lining the far wall. The large store, built onto the end of a row of shops, featured an open greenhouse area in the back that was crowded with a variety of bushes and flowers. "I often buy here for my clients."

Marissa gently touched the red petals of a nearby Gerber daisy. "How long have you been in the yard service industry?"

Jacob squinted as if mentally calculating the total. "Off and on, about ten years now, I'd guess."

"You must really like it."

"It's not bad. Hey, look!" Jacob fairly tugged Marissa to a display at the end of the next aisle. "Olivia loves these mini-cacti. We could have a table at the festival set up with individual cartons of dirt for kids to plant in. Some of these minis don't have sharp needles. We could set an age limit for the table."

"We could also set out gloves as a precaution. They are pretty cute." Each tiny cactus had one or more equally small blooms in red, pink or yellow sprouting from the top of the plant. "I could see Owen liking something like this. He's always digging in our flower beds with a spade." She wrinkled her nose. "I say flower bed loosely. It's seen better days."

"Kids and dirt are usually a winning combo, regardless of how worthy the flower bed." Jacob winked. "These are on sale, and I get a discount here. If you want, I can come back and buy a few flats of the cacti to store at my house."

"That'd be great. I wouldn't know what to do

with them until the festival, otherwise." Marissa stepped back as Jacob made arrangements with a salesman to reserve the cacti for pickup, then they headed back outside into the fading sunlight.

"That went well." Jacob checked his watch. "Where to next?"

Marissa pointed down the row of shops. "We could check out the party supply store. It's right around the corner."

They headed in that direction. "Any suggestions for Olivia's big day?" Marissa asked. As hectic as her schedule was, she was looking forward to helping make the birthday girl's party a hit. Girl parties were usually more involved, but also more fun—probably because it gave Marissa a break from the constant little-boy-world of superheroes, worms and fire trucks in which she daily resided.

Jacob opened the door to the party store and motioned for Marissa to walk in first. "Olivia's mom—Liz—suggested anything pink, frilly or princess. Pretty much everything I know nothing about." He snorted. "If she wanted a superhero, however, I'd be her man."

Marissa grabbed a shopping basket and led Jacob toward the far right section of the store where the girlier items were located. "Closet comic book fan, huh?"

He offered a guilty grin, pausing to examine a box full of old-fashioned Slinky toys. "It's not that big a secret. My coworkers tease me all the time whenever a new superhero movie comes out."

She could see that. After all, Jacob already possessed a superhero vibe, playing the role of rescuer to his brother's family and even saving her from a lonely Friday night.

But his potential hero status had nothing to do with the party plans in question, and she'd only get in trouble following that line of thought. She led the way past the balloon counter. Interesting that he referred to his lawn service employees as coworkers. Such humility, if that's what it was, would certainly be a refreshing attribute in a man. Not that it mattered—Jacob was her client.

So why was she constantly reminding herself of that fact?

She shook her head to clear it, trying to focus on their conversation instead of on her own wayward thoughts. "Hey, there's nothing wrong with superheroes. Owen would attest to that."

"I don't think Olivia would agree. She's easy to please, but evil villains and red capes at her party is pushing it." He chuckled.

They rounded the corner and were suddenly surrounded by pink fluff. Jacob threw his arms up to shield his face in an exaggerated, dramatic duck. "Yikes, it's the princess row."

"Nothing on this aisle bites, I promise." Marissa laughed, swatting his arm. "It's the right decision, trust me. Girls Olivia's age usually love a princess theme, and there are a ton of options for games and food. It's a win-win."

Jacob picked up a plastic jeweled tiara. "I guess you're right. Every girl—or woman, for that matter—deserves to be a princess for a day."

Their gazes collided and lingered before Marissa quickly looked away. Did she agree? Princess for a day—nice concept for a seven-year-old, not so realistic for a single mother. She lifted her chin, hoping to steer the conversation back on course and away from the heavy. "So, princess theme it is?"

"Princess theme it is." Jacob picked up a sparkly fairy wand from a box on the shelf. "What about some of these?" He waved it through the air, sending a shower of glitter cascading to the floor. "On second thought, Liz might kill me—or even worse, make me vacuum after the party is over."

Marissa took the wand and replaced it on the shelf. "I actually already have some less glittery versions of these in my leftover-prop box at the office, along with some other things the girls will like." She smiled. "The biggest problem with this party is going to be narrowing down my list of ideas."

"Good. I was hoping this would be easy, since I railroaded you into the short-notice favor."

Marissa shook her head as she paused in front

of a huge display of stickers. "No, trust me—you're doing me the favor by letting me host the fundraiser on your land." She tossed several packages of princess stickers into the basket she held. "Speaking of, we should probably plan a time for me to see your property. I need a visual of the layout so I can get things moving for the festival."

"Good idea. Let me check my schedule." Jacob pulled out his phone and clicked a few buttons. His eyes skimmed the contents. "How's Monday around one-thirty?"

Marissa set the basket on the floor, then plucked her day planner from her purse. "Fine with me." She made a quick notation. "That would give me plenty of time before I need to pick up Owen from school."

Jacob gestured to the planner. "Does that thing travel everywhere with you?"

"Everywhere. It's funny, I got used to carrying Owen's diaper bag for so many years that when he got older, I kept feeling like I was forgetting something every time I left the house." She tucked it back inside her purse. "This is my new security blanket."

"Well, I just admitted I'm a comic fan, so your secret is safe with me."

Safe. Now, there was a concept. Marissa risked a glance into his eyes, now a darker blue, as he picked up the basket from the floor and handed it to her. The teasing lilt had left his gaze, replaced with something deeper.

"I don't want a train party! I want a zoo party!" A child in the next aisle screamed a tantrum, and Marissa jerked, losing the moment. Or had she only imagined the chemistry sizzling between them?

"At least she's a young woman who knows what she wants." Jacob nodded toward the commotion with a laugh. "Hey, how about feather boas?"

"Of course. Grab the purple ones, too." Marissa sneaked a glance at Jacob's profile as he draped the boas into the basket. There was something incredibly endearing about watching a grown man pick out and handle little-girl toys.

She wished she could recapture the moment they'd shared before the distraction from the next row shattered it with reality. But as the parent in the next aisle knew all too well, reality came with being a mom. There was a reason fairy tale princesses didn't have children—it wasn't always happily ever after and romance. Maybe the interruption had been for the best. Anything other than a business relationship would be a joke. Marissa was a mommy first and entrepreneur second, with little room for a third label.

Even if for the first time since Kevin's death, she sort of wanted one.

* * *

The wind teased the edges of Marissa's blond hair and blew several strands across her cheek as they ambled toward the parking garage. Jacob wished he could brush them back, but the night had gone so well, he wasn't about to mess it up now with something that forward. The moon cut a path between the clouds, providing them with a momentary spotlight before they walked under the cover of the concrete garage.

After leaving the party store, they'd gotten burgers and ice cream cones and sat outside on a bench by the river to eat. In between bites, they talked about Owen, Marissa's business, Jacob's brother and family, and various plans for the upcoming festival. The more they talked, the better they connected, bouncing ideas off each other and feeding upon the other's creativity. The longer he remained in Marissa's presence, the more he felt like he'd known her forever.

"Where'd you park?" He scanned the almost empty bottom level of the garage, a reminder of how late the evening had gotten—and how quickly it had passed.

"I think…over there? My sense of direction isn't the best." Marissa pointed toward the back with a shrug. "It's sort of a guessing game every time I leave a restaurant or the mall. Owen usually remembers better than I do."

Jacob grinned. "Then let's see how you did without him." He led the way, unable to help but picture several more nights exactly like this one—maybe next time holding hands or bringing Owen along for a ride on the two-story carousal. If the kid was anything like his mother, he had to be one amazing little boy.

What would it be like to have a family of his own? Sure, there would be fights and tantrums, like the little girl displayed in the party store, but the good times would outweigh the bad. Hanging out with Ryan, Liz and Olivia reminded Jacob of his desire for his own family more and more lately—and everything about him and Marissa seemed to mesh. They had several things in common—their mutual love for kids, the outdoors and double-scoop ice cream cones—but enough differences between them to keep the conversation interesting. She was a great mom—that much was obvious in the way her eyes sparkled as she told stories of Owen's antics—not to mention a confident businesswoman.

And there was no question she was beautiful.

They reached Marissa's SUV, and Jacob paused beside it. "I almost didn't recognize it without a flat tire."

Marissa laughed as she stashed their shopping bags into the backseat. "Let's hope that was a one-time thing." She checked her watch and grimaced.

"I better hurry. I told Owen's babysitter I'd be back by nine."

Jacob opened the driver's door for her and grinned. "Mommy to the rescue." He supposed dating Marissa—if she ever even agreed to a real date—would be like that. Owen came first, and he had absolutely no problem with the fact. He'd actually be upset if that wasn't the case.

"Thanks for asking me here." Marissa fumbled with her car keys. "I'm, uh—really looking forward to working with you."

A truck rumbled down their row, and Jacob eased a step closer to be heard over the noise— or so he told himself. "So am I." He held out his hand to assist her into the driver's seat, and fought the urge to let his grip linger. *Don't rush it,* his conscience whispered a warning, and he pulled free before his fingers refused to obey. But he couldn't pass up the chance to ask Marissa out. Who knew when he'd get another one? He hesitated, then braced one arm against the door to keep it open. "Would you like to do this again sometime?"

"Shop and eat junk food?" A teasing spark lit her eyes, and he thought for the hundredth time how beautiful she was.

"If you want." Jacob smiled back. "But I was thinking about something a little more official." He swallowed. If he'd read her signals wrong and she said no, then he had just officially made their working relationship awkward. But he had to know.

Surprise lit Marissa's deep green eyes, and he could almost read the conflicting emotions darting across her expression. Interest. Doubt. Regret. Which would win? He waited, a knot slowly forming in his stomach.

"That would be...nice."

Jacob let out his breath, unable to decipher who was more surprised by her answer—him or her. But regardless, he'd take it.

"Great." He lowered his arm as she inserted the key into the wheel, the ignition dinging. "We'll talk about that soon." Very soon.

"I'd like that." They smiled, then Marissa broke the connection as she pulled on her seat belt. "If I haven't said so yet, this is a great thing you're doing for the families of the laid off firemen. They're going to appreciate it a lot."

"It's nothing much. My brother deserves a break after the layoffs. I only wish I could do more." He could never do enough to ease the guilt he felt, but he'd go down trying.

"Wait—the fire department layoff?" Marissa tilted her head to one side in surprise.

Jacob blinked. "I didn't mention that before now? Ryan was one of the firemen let go. That's why I'm helping out with Olivia's party."

"No, you never mentioned the specifics, just that he was suddenly unemployed. Wow, I'm sorry to hear that." Admiration flickered in Marissa's gaze. "But I'm sure your helping with the fundraiser will encourage your brother. Family support is so important."

"I hope so. None of the guys deserved this." Jacob's stomach tightened. It had been like losing family after the first round of cuts. The worst part was that rumor had it the city council wasn't done yet. But no need to stir up the bitterness when tonight had gone so well. Come to think of it, had he even mentioned he was a fireman? They'd talked about the party, the fundraiser and Owen and Olivia most of the night.

Marissa started the engine with a roar, interrupting his thoughts. "I wish everyone was as supportive of the fundraiser as you are—like my dad, for instance." She raised her voice above the rumble.

He knew she needed to leave, but now he was confused. Why would her father not care about the affected firemen and their families? How could any civilian not care? Ever since the layoffs, the local newspapers had been flooded with letters to the editor about their concerns. He couldn't imagine someone feeling the opposite. "What do you mean, your dad?"

She gripped the steering wheel with both hands. "Fire Chief Brady."

Jacob's heart slammed against his rib cage with a catastrophic jolt.

"He says it's a conflict of interest for me to be involved, but I believe it's the right thing to do. Not only for my business, but as a person. I just couldn't turn down the church when they asked." She kept talking but her words rushed straight over Jacob's head and into the stifling air of the garage as he desperately tried to comprehend this new truth. Chief Brady. His boss. Marissa's father. Marissa Brady Hawthorne.

"Oh, no, it's nine o'clock now. I'll see you Monday afternoon." Marissa held up her hand in a quick wave. "Good night."

"Good night." The words croaked from Jacob's tight throat as the SUV door slammed shut between them.

Then she was gone.

Chapter Four

Marissa punched the button in her SUV to open the garage door, her headlights piercing the late evening darkness and reminding her how badly she needed to power-wash the house. Usually such chores only served as a gateway into overwhelming reminders of how she didn't have backup any-more—no man around to take out the trash or mow the yard, no husband to change burned out lightbulbs, check the oil in her car or get rid of scary bugs in the bathroom.

But tonight, for the first time in a while, the familiar cloak of regret didn't settle itself around her shoulders. Instead, an image of Jacob chasing a fly around her living room flitted through her mind, and she shook her head with a grin. Not even one official date behind them, and already she fantasized about the poor man doing grunt work. But with the way he so easily fit into her imagination, it felt as if she'd already known him forever.

She sneaked a peek in her rearview mirror at Owen, sound asleep in the back. He'd had a fun night with his friend from school, and Mrs. Johnson hadn't minded her being late at all. "You need to get out more, enjoy life." The middle-aged woman's soft voice prodded Marissa's conscience as she helped buckle Owen into the backseat. "You're a mom, Marissa, but you're still a woman who deserves to have fun. I'm glad you seem to be remembering that again."

Mrs. Johnson must have misunderstood, since the evening was simply a business meeting. But Jacob still provided Marissa with a much-needed reminder of how nice it was to be treated like a lady, not just a boss, a friend or a parent. The way he insisted on opening doors for her and letting her walk first, the way he'd looked into her eyes as if what she said really meant something, proved there were still bona fide gentlemen in Orchid Hill after all. He even listened to her talk about her business and Owen for a good portion of the evening as if there were nothing else he'd rather hear. It was a refreshing change.

One she could get used to.

Marissa inched her SUV into the dark garage and powered the door closed behind them. She twisted around in her seat, mouth open to wake Owen, but the words faded on her lips. Her son slept peacefully, one hand tucked under his cheek, a swatch of hair crowding his forehead and his other hand holding one end of the fire truck he'd been determined to take with him.

Moments like these were few and far between lately. "You're growing up fast." Her whisper, so soft she could barely hear it, lingered in the air between them like a benediction. One of the greatest tragedies of Kevin's death was Owen losing a father figure. No one could ever replace Kevin in Owen's life, but he needed a positive male influence. Unfortunately, it didn't look as if Owen could get that from his grandfather, either.

Marissa smiled wistfully as Owen stirred into a more comfortable position. Maybe she'd been depriving Owen in the long run by devoting all her time to her business, trying to guarantee financial security instead of taking time to date and find her son a potential stepfather. Maybe it was hurting Owen that she avoided the social scene and rarely took time to fill her own emotional needs. But wasn't that part of being a good mom?

Too heavy a topic to think about after such a wonderful evening.

Marissa climbed out and opened Owen's door, unbuckled his seat belt and tried to remove the fire truck from his grip. At least tonight had been a distraction from the argument with her father at his office, and the anger she still felt simmering in her stomach whenever she thought of a busybody fireman trying to influence her son into a career she dreaded. The familiar wave of indignation washed over her at the memory, and she shook her head to clear it. No sense in ending the night with sour thoughts. Those issues would keep until tomorrow.

"Wake up, buddy." She jostled Owen's shoulder. He stirred again, but didn't wake up. Marissa shook a little harder, wishing she was strong enough to carry him to bed like she did years before. Owen muttered in his sleep, then flung his arm sideways, clocking her in the side of the head with the fire truck.

Marissa jerked upright, biting back the frustration that rushed to her lips. She closed her eyes and rubbed the offended spot on her head as Owen let out a fresh snore.

She *really* didn't like that truck.

Jacob loved fire trucks. Even on days like today when he was stuck washing them, he couldn't help but admire what the trucks symbolized. Rescue. Redemption. This one vehicle could do everything from putting out a fire that threatened to consume someone's life and belongings, to stretching a ladder into a tree to rescue a family pet. Of course, the latter was typically more annoying than the former, especially at 2:00 a.m., but he never tired of seeing a child's face light up at the return of a furry friend.

Besides, focusing on how much he loved his job distracted him from the memory of Marissa's smile.

Jacob dropped his sponge back into the bucket of sudsy water and reached for the garden hose. "Crank it," he hollered from the driveway outside the bay to Steve. He waited for the water to gurgle, then aimed the green tube at the top of the truck. Water gushed out and Jacob wiped his sweating forehead with his shirtsleeve as he sprayed. Try as he might, he couldn't erase the dreaded repeat of Marissa's words at the end of last night. "My dad—Fire Chief Brady." The simple sentence pulverized his brain until he could barely think straight. Of all the dads in all of the world, why did hers have to be his boss?

His boss, who not even a year ago made life so miserable for one of the men on Jacob's shift, that the guy finally requested a transfer—all because of an overheard crude comment about his daughter. Chief Brady played by the rules of the union and their laws about seniority, but if he needed those rules bent for his own purposes, he wasn't above stretching whatever lines he could—hence the reason his old coworker was now in Baton Rouge instead of Orchid Hill. No, offending Chief Brady wasn't a good idea—and one of his firemen dating his only daughter was sure to be considered offensive, even if Jacob's intentions were more honorable than his coworker's lewd comment.

Well, make that former intentions.

Jacob leveled the hose at the truck tires, and mentally kicked himself for not connecting the dots sooner. He'd known the chief's daughter's name was Marissa, but since she obviously still went by her married last name, he had no reason to assume it was the same woman he'd taken out last night.

Disappointment sucker punched Jacob's stomach like a heavy fist. How was he going to help plan Olivia's birthday party and host the Fireman's Festival with Marissa, knowing he could look but never touch? Last night in the parking garage, he'd asked Marissa on a real date. Now he was going to have to forego on his word, something he hated to do, all because the world was much, much too small.

Jacob drew a tight breath in an attempt to battle his frustration. "Okay, kill it." He waited for Steve to shut off the water, but several moments passed and it continued to spew from the hose. "Steve! I said kill it." If his coworker had gone back inside to catch the end of the soccer game on TV... Jacob's frustration, combined with the heat of the sun beating down on his head and neck, boiled over and he stomped around the far end of the truck with the hose. "Steve! Where did—"

He stopped short, nearly running into a pair of shiny black boots and starched white dress shirt, as the water continued to pour.

Straight onto Fire Chief Brady.

Jacob watched any chances of pursuing Marissa's heart drip off the top of Chief's hat and onto his pressed pants. "Chief Brady, I am so sorry. I didn't see you." He opened his mouth to apologize further but clamped it shut as the chief removed his wet black sunglasses.

"I suppose that's what I get for making a surprise visit." He rubbed the lenses on his shirt, but they were so wet that it didn't seem to help. He smiled, but in the afternoon sun it came across more as a grimace.

Jacob suddenly realized the hose was still gushing water, now down the driveway toward the street. He quickly dropped it and jogged to the faucet on the side of the brick station. With a quick yank, he stopped the flow. The sudden quiet seemed overwhelming. Chief pointedly cleared his throat.

"Let me get you a towel." Jacob headed into the bay, mortification heating his neck hotter than the sunburn he could feel tingling the tips of his ears. A hand towel from the station kitchen wouldn't do much good, but he couldn't stand there staring at the chief's undershirt beneath his uniform any longer.

He snagged a towel and brought it to the chief, who had followed him to the front door of the station. Steve jumped off the couch and shut off the soccer game with a quick click of the remote control. Jacob shot him a glare. He owed Jacob—kitchen duty for a month, at least. Though, come to think of it, that might be more a punishment on Jacob's part.

Captain Walker breezed in from his office by the kitchen, did a double take at Chief Brady standing in the doorway patting his neck with a dish rag and raised his eyebrows at Jacob. Jacob shook his head.

"Afternoon, Chief. What brings you by?" Captain Walker extended one arm to offer the chief access inside, then hesitated at the puddle forming by the older man's boots on the concrete walk.

Steve snorted back a laugh, and Jacob elbowed his ribs.

"Come on in. My boys will handle the mess, don't worry." Captain Walker gestured to the chief, confusion puzzling his brow.

"That's all right. I need to get back and get a fresh uniform now." Chief Brady handed over the wet towel. "I'm heading to each station to give notice in person that we've received more emails from locals upset about the layoffs."

Jacob's back stiffened and he shifted his weight, hoping to hide the obvious frustration welling in his chest. Did the chief know Jacob by his full name? Would he immediately connect the fact that his brother was one of the firefighters let go?

Or worse yet, that he had taken his daughter out to the Boardwalk last night? He swallowed.

"Threatening emails?" Captain Walker rested one hand against the door frame. "Or angry citizens blowing smoke?"

"Some of each. Let's keep an eye out in case things get violent. If there's any suspicious activity around the station, let me know immediately. One of our men's personal vehicles at Station 3 was broken into last night, but Captain May seems to think it's unrelated."

"What do you think?" The words jumped from Jacob's lips before he could stop them, and he inwardly groaned at drawing attention to himself.

Chief's chin lifted a fraction, a typically intimidating pose but less effective with a soggy collar. "I'm keeping all options open."

Jacob nodded. "Yes, sir."

Captain Walker's eyes narrowed at Jacob, then he turned back to the chief with a tight smile. "Are you sure you don't want another towel? One for your car's seat?"

"I'll manage." Chief Brady lifted one hand in

a wave before disappearing back down the driveway to the department vehicle parked on the curb.

Captain shut the door with a solid thud. "Anyone care to explain why the chief is wet and a water hose is sprawled across the front lawn?"

Steve pointed at Jacob, and Jacob brushed aside his hand. "That's a long story, Captain." He hesitated. "But the trucks are clean."

"So is Chief Brady's bald spot." Captain rubbed his temples with both fingers, then pointed at Jacob. "You. Outside. Clean up." He pointed at Steve. "You. Kitchen. Clean up."

"Yes, sir." Jacob and Steve spoke in unison as they headed in opposite directions. Grateful the chief had already driven away, Jacob began rolling the hose back onto the mounted holder. Threatening emails. A car broken into at work. Were the incidents related? Was someone seeking revenge for one of the laid off men? Of course it was wrong, but he could understand the anger behind it. Ryan had worked hard to provide for his family, put in all he had for a job he assumed would be his lifelong career and then *bam*. It was all taken away because of the mayor and city council's lack of ability to properly manage city funds—all while they continued to drive their city-funded cars and received cost-of-living raises. It wasn't fair, and while Jacob knew that life lesson all too well, it didn't ease the pain he felt for his family.

He tucked the end of the hose out of sight and wiped his damp hands on his pants, then stared down the street where the chief had just driven away. All the more reason to stay far away from Marissa Hawthorne. Jacob didn't need any reason to upset Chief Brady or create an opportunity to lose his own job. If he did, how would Ryan and his family manage without his financial support? How would *he* manage?

There was only one problem. Marissa Hawthorne was coming to his house Monday afternoon to check out his land for the festival, and unless she'd had as rough a weekend as his, she would probably be just as gorgeous as ever.

Despite the tilt of her smile, the laughter in her Southern drawl, and the way her eyes shone when she talked about the things she loved—he couldn't allow himself to fall one inch further than he'd already slipped.

He climbed into the truck and inserted the key in the ignition, pausing to rest his forehead against the steering wheel. *God, I thought she had come into my life for a reason—but I was obviously wrong. Help me get through this without messing it up for my family.* He started the truck, then closed his eyes briefly. *And if You could somehow have Chief Brady forget about the water hose incident today, that'd be great.*

He checked the mirrors before inching his way

into the bay, but all he saw was Marissa's smile. He shook his head to clear it and backed up another few feet. Jacob already had one wet strike on his record now.

He couldn't risk a second.

Chapter Five

Monday morning brought fresh determination—and a little bit of despair. Marissa stared at her day planner and shook her head. Maybe she shouldn't have agreed to the birthday party after all. She wanted to help, but how could she concentrate on glittery wands and princess snacks when she still had to arrange all the fundraiser vendors—both food and games—brainstorm craft projects for the kids, book an inflatable jumping booth, find volunteers from the church to man all the booths, order the tickets, find someone willing to stand in a tent all day and *sell* tickets…

The hastily scribbled notes on the page of her planner blurred before Marissa's tired eyes. Perhaps after she saw Jacob's property this afternoon, some of the details would fall together in her head. It was hard to plan without being able to picture the space she had to work with. In the meantime, she should focus on the birthday party since that wasn't depending on anything else. She shut the file and reached for the party folder just as the front door of Your Special Day swung open.

"Good morning." A short, curly-haired brunette stepped inside with a hesitant smile. "You're open, right?"

"Hi, there. Yes, I'm open." Marissa glanced at the clock. Was it still early? Nope, it was nine-thirty—already. So far she'd accomplished nothing other than giving herself a mild stress headache. "How can I help you?" She folded her hands across the planner, hoping any event the woman wanted to plan would be at least a month away. She hated to turn away a new client.

The brunette paused by the bookshelf of party theme books by the door and tilted her head to read the title on a spine. "I'm Liz Greene." She looked up and gave a sheepish shrug. "You're planning my daughter's birthday party."

"You're Jacob's sister-in-law?" Marissa stood with a smile. "It's so nice to meet you! Come sit down." She gestured to the chair across from her desk. "I've already got some ideas I'd love to run by you."

Liz perched on the edge of the seat. "That sounds good. Jacob explained how bad he felt about the short notice."

"It's no problem." Marissa followed Liz's gaze

taking in the stacks of files on her desk. "Okay, so it's a little bit of a problem, but honestly, I would have felt worse saying no. Especially after what your family is going through with the layoff."

"It's been hard, to say the least. But we're hanging in there." Liz leaned back against the chair with a sigh. "It makes us get creative financially, that's for sure."

"I can imagine." Marissa tapped the folder on her desk. "I can't do much, but I am planning the fireman's fundraiser, and I'm also determined to make sure your daughter has one of the best birthdays she's ever had." Her earlier hesitations about the party fled at the grateful expression on Liz's face. As a mom, Marissa could easily empathize. If she lost her job, of course she would still want Owen to be taken care of and enjoy his birthday. None of this was Liz's fault. "Jacob agreed to my suggestion of a princess party. How does that sound?"

"Perfect!" Liz relaxed in her chair, crossing her jean-clad legs. "Olivia is a sweet girl, very easy to please. I told Jacob he didn't have to do this, that she'd be perfectly happy with some stickers and store-bought cupcakes, but he insisted." Liz grinned. "He's a good brother-in-law, even though he's somewhat stubborn."

Marissa rolled in her lower lip but couldn't keep the smile from her eyes.

"You look as if you already knew that." Liz raised a thin eyebrow.

"That's a long story." Marissa waved one hand to change the subject, embarrassment flushing her neck. She couldn't get all moony about Jacob in front of his family. No doubt it'd get back to Jacob, and then how would she come across? Not professional.

Though, there was nothing professional about checking her cell phone every thirty minutes to make sure he hadn't called to schedule their official date.

"If you say so." Liz's eyebrow remained arched, but she changed the subject. "Well, listen, I don't want to keep you, but I came to say thank you for agreeing to plan this party, and the fundraiser. It's been amazing how the community has stepped up to help, and I want to give back. So, if you need extra help around here, please call me."

"Don't be silly." Marissa shook her head. "You're one of the families the fundraiser is hoping to help. This whole thing is for you—and your husband."

"All the more reason why I should be involved and contribute." Liz slid a card with her name and phone number across the desk to Marissa. "I mean it. I want to help."

Marissa tucked the card in the designated slot in her planner, her elbow accidentally catching one of the files on her desk. It wobbled precariously and Liz jumped from the chair to balance the stack.

"You know what?" Marissa grinned. "I think I might take you up on that offer after all."

Marissa made the final turn onto Jacob's street and flipped her visor down to shield her eyes from the sun. Beams of light spiraled between tall, leafy pine trees and streaked the dashboard with gold. She pulled into a long driveway and parked several yards back from a simple, pier-and-beams style house with a wraparound porch. The yard had been recently mowed, and the flower beds neatly tended. Of course the owner of a lawn service would have well-kept property—and judging by the land sprawling on each side of the house, business must be pretty good to afford this much acreage.

She got out of her SUV and shut the door with her hip, turning a slow circle to take in the details of the land. The driveway seemed to split the property in half, which was perfect. There would be plenty of space on each side for a mini-carnival and a designated parking area for guests. It was laid out even better than she could have hoped.

The screen door opened onto the porch, and Jacob stepped out, wearing jeans and a white T-shirt. He looked right at home in the casual wear, and she couldn't contain the grin spreading across her face. "Hi, there." It'd only been three days since their evening on the Boardwalk, but it felt like too long. Maybe this afternoon he'd make good on his invitation to plan a date. Anticipation simmered in Marissa's stomach and she lifted her hand in a wave.

"Afternoon." Jacob made his way down the stairs toward the driveway, passing a fireman's flag stuck in the corner of the flower bed. Her dad kept the same one in his front yard for years. Jacob must have been very proud of his brother to have one. Would he remove the flag now that his sibling had been laid off?

"Did you find the place all right?" Jacob's question jerked her from her thoughts.

"Yes, your directions were great." Marissa clenched her purse strap in one fist as he drew near, feeling silly now for not stopping at the house to change clothes first. She still wore her heels and dress pants from the office, and they were about to go on the equivalent of a hike. But she'd gladly wobble around on high heels for the chance to visit with Jacob. She'd even arranged for her mother to pick up Owen from school today, just so she wouldn't have to rush. They had a lot to cover for the fundraiser, and if they ended up talking as much as they had last Friday, then she'd need all the time she could get.

"Good." He stopped several feet away from her and focused on a spot somewhere over her shoulder. She looked, but saw nothing worthy of his devoted attention. She turned back with a puzzled frown.

"I saw your sister-in-law today." Marissa stretched on tiptoe, angling sideways to try to catch his eye. "She came into the store."

"Liz did?" Jacob's gaze collided with hers. "What did she say?"

Marissa blinked rapidly at the clipped, nearly defensive words. "She said she was grateful for all you were doing for them, and all the community was doing. She offered to help me in the office with the grunt work, if I needed it."

"Oh, right. Yeah, Liz is nice like that." Jacob shook his head as if clearing it. "Well, this is it." He gestured to the property. "Think it will work?"

The warmth from Friday night was missing in his voice, leaving a stilted, businesslike tone instead. What happened? Marissa crossed both arms in front of her chest, confused and more than a little defensive. "Yes, I think it will work well."

Jacob nodded, hands in his pockets now, his back stiff. Something was obviously wrong, judging by the tick in his jaw.

Marissa brushed a piece of hair from her face that had come loose from her ponytail and faced him, holding one hand up to her eyes against the sun. "Is everything okay?"

He nodded again.

"Bad day?" That much was obvious, but maybe the acknowledgment would encourage him to explain.

He opened his mouth, closed it, then said, "Why don't we look at the area behind the house? I was thinking we should set up an arts and crafts area for the kids, and that might be a good spot."

He'd obviously rather talk about glue guns and glitter than whatever was bothering him, so Marissa bit back the argument on her tongue and followed him around the porch.

"They could set up here." He pointed toward the tree line. "Out of the way of foot traffic, but still easily accessible."

Marissa pulled out her pen and planner and made a notation. "Good idea. Thanks."

Thumbs hooked in his jeans pockets, Jacob looked off toward the red barn that sat about an acre back to the left. An open outbuilding beside the barn served as a covering for two trailers, probably the ones he carted his lawn mowers on. "So what else do you need?"

Was he in that big of a hurry for her to leave? Frustration and confusion burned the back of her throat, and she found it difficult to meet his eyes. Not that he was giving her much chance of that anyway. Obviously, whatever expectations she had for her time with him today were far from accurate. She must have misunderstood his intentions Friday night. But he asked her out—officially, and almost nervously as if he had really hoped she'd agree. How else was that to be interpreted?

"I guess that's it." Marissa turned back toward the driveway and her car, angry at herself for allowing the waver in her voice. "I better head back into town before Owen gets out of school." She could call her mom on the way home and cancel their plans, although Owen would be disappointed not to see his nana. But at least if Marissa got him from school herself she could avoid seeing her dad tonight when she picked up Owen. Another verbal round with him was the last way she wanted to end this rotten afternoon.

"Marissa, wait."

She hesitated at Jacob's voice, but didn't stop. She had enough of his bad mood for today. Maybe if she left without revealing her hurt, it wouldn't cause awkwardness between them later. "I should go." She stuffed her planner in her purse and grabbed for her keys. They fell on the gravel drive, and Jacob scooped them up before she could bend over.

"You were right. It's been a bad day." He blew out a short breath and attempted a smile. "I didn't mean to be rude."

Her hopes rose. If he was simply having a rough afternoon, then he wasn't upset with her personally after all. Perhaps he wasn't trying to back out of their future date and she was just being paranoid. After all, Kevin had been moody most of their marriage. Jacob was allowed a bad day or two.

"Want to talk about it?" Marissa swallowed, trying to decide how much of her hopes to risk. Her hand shook, but she had to know. They'd had such a great time together last weekend—surely there was a chance they could do so again. She bit her lower lip. Finding out would be better than wondering—right? She hesitated, then blurted the words before she could change her mind. "Maybe over that dinner date you mentioned Friday?"

Jacob's smile slowly faded. "About that…" He coughed. "Look, Marissa, I'm sorry, but I can't—"

"It's okay." She cut him off before he could fully verbalize the rejection, her hopes shattering like the perfume bottle Owen had dropped on the bathroom tile last month. She straightened her shoulders, determined to remain professional. "Thanks for letting me see the property."

"Anytime." Emotion darkened Jacob's eyes, a contradiction to the words he'd just spoken. Did he regret them?

Confused, Marissa took the keys he held out in his palm, ignoring the jolt of electricity that still occurred on contact. She quickly opened the door of her SUV and climbed inside. This time, he didn't stay to shut her door as he had Friday night. He simply turned and ambled toward the front porch, head down, shoulders slumped.

She turned around in the grassy spot by the carport, unwilling to risk backing out of the long driveway all the way to the road.

And unwilling to risk one more portion of her heart on Jacob Greene.

Jacob pulled back the blinds and watched Marissa drive down the gravel drive, hoping the hand she brushed across her face was shoving aside loose hair and not a tear. He didn't know what hurt worse—the fact that he'd been borderline rude to the least deserving woman on the planet, or the fact that she probably thought he was a complete jerk now.

He dropped the blinds as her SUV disappeared from sight, and stalked to the fridge. His one rare day off that he wasn't working at the station or working on a yard, and he was going to spend it miserable because he couldn't tell Marissa the truth.

Well, he could—but would it sound presumptuous to tell her they couldn't date because of her dad? Because of the domino effect a relationship would have not only on his career but on his family's welfare?

Although after today, she wouldn't want to date him anyway.

He grabbed a carton of orange juice and took a swig, the cool liquid doing little to calm his frustration. In answer to his own question, it wouldn't be presumptuous at all—Marissa was obviously expecting him to keep his word about another date, or she wouldn't have hinted about it when she asked if he wanted to talk. He should have told her right then and there. But it was all he could do not to wrap her in a hug at the sadness in her gaze.

Sadness he'd placed there.

He slammed the refrigerator door and rested both hands on the countertop. It didn't help that Liz had gone by the store today to introduce herself to Marissa. If those two were going to be working together in the office, things would surely go from bad to very bad. The last thing he needed was a meddler in this hairy situation, and Liz was well known for her matchmaking ways. At least Liz didn't seem to have mentioned that he was a fireman when she stopped by Your Special Day.

It'd be easier if Liz had spilled the proverbial beans, but he couldn't let that happen. Marissa deserved the truth from him. After all, he was the one who let things move as far as they had in their relationship, risking a professional relationship for something more. It was his fault it couldn't happen now, and therefore his responsibility to explain.

One thing was certain, though—ignoring the obvious wasn't going to be an option anymore. Not with the way Jacob's heart pounded in Marissa's presence and her smile wreaked havoc on his stomach. He'd hoped he'd be able to keep a professional distance today as he would have with any other party planner, but the minute she'd stepped out of the car, he realized that wasn't going to happen.

If they had any chance of working together on the fundraiser and the party for his niece, they were going to have to talk. Awkward as it might be, it would be worse to let things remain unexplained and Marissa wrongfully assume he was no longer interested in her.

Jacob drew a deep breath, certain he could still smell the lingering aroma of Marissa's lilac perfume.

No, interest was not the problem.

Chapter Six

"I've got four volunteers to manage the ticket booth for the festival." Liz hung up the office phone and made a bold check mark beside an item on the list Marissa had given her earlier that day. "They said they'll alternate shifts."

Marissa made her own check mark in her planner. "Wow, that's great. I haven't been able to find anyone willing to do the grunt work yet." She grinned. "Where have you been all my life?"

Liz laughed, the sound contagious and uplifting like the rest of Liz's personality. "Raising a kid?"

"I hear you on that one." Marissa stood from her desk chair and stretched. They'd been making calls for the fundraiser for nearly two hours straight. Judging by the accomplishments on Marissa's list, the effort had been well worth it.

At least staying busy had been a distraction from the disappointment of seeing Jacob yesterday.

It'd been hard not to quiz Liz about her brother-in-law in between their long talks about family and children throughout the day. Maybe Liz would have some insight into Jacob's sudden mood swing. But it didn't feel right to ask. Marissa had no claim on Jacob, despite her heart insisting otherwise. She'd only look foolish.

"Need some water?" Marissa opened the dorm fridge beside her desk and removed two cold bottles.

"Sounds good." Liz caught the bottle Marissa tossed and unscrewed the cap. "It's already almost three-thirty. The kids should be here soon."

Both women had arranged for a joint carpool to drop Olivia and Owen at the shop today so they could continue making progress on the festival for as long as possible. Marissa glanced at her watch. "You're right. Today sure has gone by fast. I'm really glad you came in."

"I told you I would." Liz took a sip of her water. "I'm good at convincing people to do things they don't normally want to do." She winked.

"Aren't all mothers?" Marissa laughed.

"Seriously, though, my church has been great about volunteering, and I knew they would be. They needed to become more aware of the need, that's all." Liz lifted one shoulder in a shrug. "They're nice people—some more stubborn than others."

Marissa nodded as the dots slowly connected. "So you go to the same church as Jacob?"

Liz hesitated with her bottle halfway to her lips. "Did I just imply my brother-in-law is stubborn?"

"You actually said as much yesterday when you first came to my store." At the time, the statement from Liz had brought a smile and a feeling of bonding as Marissa had begun getting to know Jacob as well. Now it made Marissa feel like an outsider to a family joke—a family she obviously wouldn't get to become close to, other than perhaps through her new friendship with Liz.

"As I recall, you didn't really seem all that surprised." Liz smirked.

"No—well, not now anyway. Although, I'm not sure if stubborn is the right word." Marissa screwed the lid back on her water bottle and set it on her desk. It was probably her fault. She'd been out of the dating world longer than most, and there was still the chance she had misunderstood Jacob's intentions. But why else would he have asked her on a date? Something changed between Friday night, when she left the Boardwalk, and Monday afternoon, when she arrived at his house. The question remained—what? They'd had zero contact over the weekend. How could she have offended him if they hadn't spoken?

"I don't have any pennies, but I can offer you a peppermint for your thoughts." With a grin, Liz reached into the pocket of her denim capri pants. "Olivia's favorite."

"It's…nothing." Unfortunately nothing, which was the whole point. Marissa had allowed herself to hope, and all she'd gotten was disappointment.

One would think she'd be used to that by now.

"It's something, girl. Anyone can see that. The question is do you want to talk about it? If not, I'll keep my candy to myself." Liz dangled the peppermint between two fingers.

Marissa stared at the striped candy, unsure if it would cross a line to talk to Jacob's family about him—he was her client, after all. But how else would she ever find out what happened if she didn't ask? Maybe Jacob's sudden rejection was somehow a misunderstanding.

Marissa took a deep breath, her decision made. "Jacob and I went out last Friday night."

Liz's eyebrows jerked and she tossed the candy to Marissa. "Go on."

"Not on a date. We met at the Boardwalk and made some plans for the festival and for Olivia's party, and had dinner on the riverfront. Very casual."

"Sounds nice."

"It was." Marissa sighed. "That's the problem. I really had a good time, and I thought Jacob did, too. He asked me out at the end of the evening— for a real date."

"He said that?"

Marissa squinted, trying to remember his exact words. "He said he'd like to do this again sometime, but more officially. Something like that."

"That's a date." Liz nodded her confirmation. "Especially from him."

The words fell like a warning bell on Marissa's ears, but she pushed them aside to process after she finished her story. "I thought things were fine. But yesterday when I went to check out his property to see how the festival would be set up, he was weird."

"Weird?"

"Distant. Very standoffish." Humiliation swarmed Marissa's chest like a thousand tiny bee stings. "I thought he was just having a bad day, so I made some sort of reference to his asking me out."

Liz leaned forward in her chair. "And?"

The flush intensified and Marissa pressed her cold water bottle against her neck. "And he said he couldn't."

Liz's brow furrowed. "Couldn't? Not wouldn't?"

"I don't remember exactly. I wasn't in the mood to read between the lines at that point." Marissa snorted. "Although, he did seem sad when he said it—almost disappointed."

"That is strange. There's got to be something else to it."

"But nothing that you would know of?" Her last hope of explanation died with Liz's small shake of her head. Not that she expected Liz to have all the answers—but one or two would have been nice.

Marissa inhaled. "Obviously he changed his mind. I guess I need to put it out of my head and move on. He's my client, and we're working together for Olivia and for the festival, and that's what matters." The declaration sounded unconvincing, even to her own ears, and Liz's knowing gaze suggested she sensed the same.

Just then, the front door burst open and Owen and Olivia rushed inside. "Hey, buddy!" Marissa sneaked a quick hug out of Owen before waving to the carpool driver from the open door. "How was your day?"

"Great! Do you have any snacks?" Owen rushed to her desk and began rummaging through the bottom drawer, where she'd been known to keep a few stashes of candy.

Olivia, a petite little thing with long brown hair and big brown eyes, greeted her mom with a quieter hello. Liz gave her a hug, then urged her toward Marissa. "Olivia, this is the lady who is planning your party."

Marissa squatted down to her level and grinned. "It's going to be a lot of fun."

Olivia smiled back. "Will there be a pony?"

Marissa's eyes widened and she looked at Liz

over the top of the girl's head. Liz hid a laugh behind her hand, the sound coming out more like a cough. "Um, probably not a real one, but we can play pin the tail on the horse. Would that be okay?"

Olivia nodded with exuberance.

"Do you want a snack, too? I think Owen found my emergency can of Pringles."

Marissa looked over her shoulder at her son, who offered a sheepish grin as he removed the tin from her cabinet. "Learning's hard work, Mom."

"A woman who labels chips as an emergency— I'm assuming that means there's chocolate some- where else in your desk?" Liz stood up to join the hunt.

Marissa laughed. "You guys help yourselves. Try the bottom right drawer." She reached over to their assistance, when the bell on the door announced a new visitor. She turned to see Jacob filling the door frame, his navy T-shirt a stark contrast to the afternoon light behind him. Her pulse thudded in her ears and she cleared her throat. Had he come to see her? Was he going to ask her out again? Anticipation and dismay fought for full bidding in her stomach. She opened her mouth, unsure what to say, when Owen fairly squealed in excitement.

"Mom! That's the fireman who pulled a quarter from my ear at school!" Owen ran past Marissa, nearly bumping into her legs, and skidded to a stop in front of Jacob, chips spilling from the open container of Pringles still in his hand.

"Hey, little man." Jacob seemed surprised at the discovery, but crouched down and offered a high five to an excited Owen, then met Marissa's gaze.

Shock flooded Marissa's veins with every heartbeat. Jacob—a fireman? *The* unknown fireman who'd borne the brunt of her anger this past week? She searched his eyes for an explanation, fury simmering in an explosive pot in her stomach. How? Why?

Owen continued to babble on about the school safety presentation, but the words blurred together, nearly lost in the roar filling Marissa's ears.

She shook her head, willing back the sudden onslaught of angry tears threatening her vision. She couldn't lose it, not here. Not in front of her son.

Before her, Owen grinned at Jacob like a long-lost hero. "I'm going to be a fireman one day, too."

That was it. A vise clenched Marissa's heart in an unyielding grasp, and she couldn't help the daggers she bore into the side of Jacob's profile.

He must have felt her visual warning, for he slowly stood and met her gaze. "We need to talk."

She nodded once and led him to the front door, frustrated tears biting her eyes. He was right about that.

* * *

Jacob followed Marissa outside, her back a straight, rigid line in front of him. She'd wasted no time in asking Liz to keep an eye on the kids and hightailing it to the front door. Following her felt similar to what he imagined a guillotine walk would resemble. But he owed her.

He joined her outside, shutting the door firmly behind him. From the fire in Marissa's eyes, this wouldn't be a conversation the kids needed to hear. He waited for the first verbal punch, deserving that and probably more.

"You lied to me." Marissa's words, sharp with betrayal, cut a ragged hole in Jacob's emotions. But the hurt in her eyes filled the hole with regret, and was nearly his undoing.

"I didn't lie." The wind lifted Marissa's hair from her shoulders, and Jacob wanted to touch her—tuck that unruly strand of blond behind her ear, or press his fingers against her cheek—anything to convince her he was telling the truth. He knew this day was coming, knew he needed to beat Liz to revealing his career, but he never imagined it would have happened like this. He'd come over to the shop to apologize for his behavior yesterday and try to find a way to tell Marissa why he couldn't follow through with their date after all.

But Owen's involvement in the revelation of his secret wiped away any chances of keeping a friendship with Marissa—and possibly even a civil working relationship. He hadn't realized Owen was Marissa's son until a moment ago. At the elementary school when they performed the safety demonstration, he'd been focused on Olivia—he never recognized Owen from the picture on Marissa's desk, even after their classroom game with the quarter. Now, though, it seemed impossible that he couldn't have—or at least that's how it would look to Marissa. She wouldn't understand that at school, the dozens of faces tended to blur.

Now it looked like he'd been keeping secrets with her son. He didn't have to be a parent to know that was unacceptable—especially in the undefined, fledging state of their current relationship.

Marissa shifted her weight, her arms crossed tightly across her chest. "You said you owned a lawn business. Is that even true?"

"Of course—it's my side job. Most firemen have side jobs."

Her eyes narrowed. "Trust me, I know what firemen do."

That's right. Her father. Was that where all this anger was stemming from? Jacob let out a deep sigh. "My career is firefighting. I've been doing that for years alongside my lawn service." He shrugged. "It's what I do. Who I am."

"Why didn't you tell me?" Her whispered words, no longer angry but carrying a definite tinge of bitterness, were nearly swallowed up with another gust of wind. The same breeze wafted her lilac scent, the subtle aroma an assault on Jacob's resolve.

He braced himself. "It never came up. I didn't realize you hadn't known until we were leaving the Boardwalk Friday and you told me who your father was." Jacob raked his hands through his hair. "I was shocked. I had no idea you were Chief Brady's daughter. If I had known, I wouldn't have ever—" He stopped, not sure how to say the rest of that sentence without increasing her hurt. It wasn't Marissa's fault who her family was. But the fact remained he couldn't get anywhere near her. Not if he wanted to keep his job and help his family.

Marissa bit her lower lip. "Wouldn't have asked me out?"

"Right." His hands dropped to his sides in defeat. Man, this wasn't fair. Not a bit of it. But how could he risk his entire career and financial support of his brother? That wouldn't be right—even if part of him wanted to.

She nodded slowly, processing the new information, her eyes averted somewhere over his shoulder. A truck rumbled by the street to their left, and the birds chirped from nearby trees as if this was any other, regular day. But the cheery décor of Your Special Day, visible through the window behind Marissa, served as a startling contradiction to the sadness in her expression. Sadness he was once again responsible for.

Jacob couldn't help it. He reached for her hand. "Marissa, you have to believe me. I never meant for you to find out this way, never meant for Owen to get involved. I needed time to get my thoughts together, and I was going to tell you. I promise you that." He clutched her fingers in his, wishing they didn't feel so cold and lifeless.

"Seems convenient." She stared at their joined hands. Did she still feel the connection he did, despite her disappointment? But it didn't matter. It couldn't.

"Trust me, Marissa, if there was any way I could make this work—" He stopped as she abruptly tugged her hand free of his grip.

"Make what work?" Then she turned and disappeared back inside the shop, taking a portion of his heart with her.

Chapter Seven

Marissa had never felt so stupid in all her life. She blindly separated the clothes from the laundry basket, barely hearing Owen's cartoon blaring from the TV in the living room. Her thoughts littered the bedroom floor along with the haphazardly tossed items of clothing.

Pink blouse. *I should have known.* Hadn't she thought Jacob seemed familiar when she first saw him? Probably from the department picture that hung in her father's office.

Black skirt. *How could I have missed the signs?* But they'd been there. Jacob's half-finished sentences when they'd been shopping at the Boardwalk, his busy schedule trying to fit her in between two jobs, his fireman flag in the flower bed by his porch stairs.

Faded jeans. *I can't believe he lied to me.*

Logic filtered through the embarrassment as

Marissa shoved the colored pile into the washing machine. Jacob hadn't lied. Omitted, yes—but not lied. It was her own humiliation that kept that fact at bay this afternoon in the parking lot. She'd done all she could to keep from staring into Jacob's eyes, intense and fathomless like the waters of Mexico, where she cruised with Kevin years ago.

A lifetime ago.

Marissa slid to the washroom floor, her back against the dryer, and covered her face with her hands. The tears didn't come, just the too-familiar anvil of regret. Kevin had known he was in a dangerous position, running back inside that burning apartment complex despite the captain's orders. But as always, he had to be the hero.

Not for the first time, Marissa wished Kevin would have focused more on being her and Owen's hero.

She swiped her hair out of her face and drew her legs up to her chest, resting her chin on her bent knees. Some days she felt lost in a blaze, too. The pressure of being a single mom, the sole provider for Owen not only financially but emotionally as well, often resembled her own fiery furnace.

A story from Marissa's Sunday school days as a teenager teased the fringes of her mind. Hadn't there been three men in a furnace at one point in the Old Testament? God saved them, if she remembered correctly—even appearing to walk in the furnace with the men, who weren't even singed. If that was the case, then why didn't God save Kevin?

And why wasn't He saving Marissa now?

Marissa pushed herself to her feet and poured the liquid soap on top of the laundry. Maybe that was the pressure Kevin felt when he ran back inside that complex. Maybe he felt that if he didn't save the tenants, no one else would. God wouldn't.

Did Jacob feel that way, too?

She spun the knob and the washing machine roared to life with a rush of incoming water. Marissa stared at the suds forming around the clothes. The disappointment in her chest wasn't just about Jacob's career, and the influence he'd had on her son—though she would still have to deal with that later. The look of adoration in Owen's eyes when he saw Jacob at the shop earlier still tore at her heart. No, it wasn't even about Jacob keeping his career a secret, intentionally or not.

It was the realization that even if Jacob felt free to pursue a relationship with her, she never could. Not while he was a fireman. Not while he thrived on risk and danger.

Marissa slammed the washer lid shut with a bang.

Not while he was still caught up in trying to be a superhero.

* * *

Wednesday morning, the phone trilled from Marissa's desk—again—and she quickly dropped her purple highlighter to answer what had to have been the tenth call that hour. "Your Special Day." Sort of hard to find the pep she needed when her mind was anywhere but on the festival. She pasted on a smile she didn't feel, hoping it would help her voice inflection. "This is Marissa speaking." At least Liz wasn't here this morning to see her fake it. She promised to be in tomorrow—and would likely be more than a little curious after the exchange between her brother-in-law and Marissa the day before.

"Ms. Hawthorne, this is David Kincaid." His tone was friendly, yet professional. "Jacob Greene asked that I call you about hosting a booth at the upcoming Fireman's Festival. Are you still in need of sponsors?"

"Oh, yes, hi. Thanks for calling." Marissa scrambled for her planner, grateful for the air-conditioning rushing through the vent above her head and cooling her flushed cheeks. She'd almost forgotten Jacob had said he knew a few master gardeners in town and would have one of them contact her. He'd said that the night they were at the Boardwalk—back when they were speaking. Back before everything between them changed from wonderful to awful.

Hopeful to hopeless.

She forced Jacob from her mind as she picked up her pen, gripping it tighter than necessary and wishing she could squeeze away her memories in the same fashion. "Of course we're happy to have your participation at the event. Did you have something particular in mind?" She truly hoped so, as her creativity at this point was more than swallowed up in the never-ending festival details.

And her emotional personal life as of late.

"I do, in fact. I've teamed up with a local artist who specializes in landscapes and still-life portraits." Mr. Kincaid paused. "Do you know Julie Eberlin?"

Marissa squinted. "The name sounds familiar." Unfortunately, she never got much of a chance to check out the cultural offerings of Orchid Hill. With minimal babysitting options and free time, she had to be picky.

"She had an exhibit at the county fair last fall. Anyhow, we thought I could teach a workshop during the festival on gardening tips, and Ms. Eberlin had an idea to incorporate the children in attendance."

"Sounds good so far." Marissa nodded. "We're certainly hoping to slant the event toward families."

"Ms. Eberlin thought of drawing chalk squares on the road for each child or family to purchase for a low fee and decorate," Mr. Kincaid continued. "She'll be there to help, and at the end of the festival, will take a photo of all the squares, so each participant can keep a memento."

"That's a great idea. I love it." Not to mention so would the kids—and Marissa knew from experience that once the children saw those chalk squares, they'd convince their parents to buy tickets to draw in them. It was win-win. They'd be entertained and have a keepsake of the event, and more important, tickets would be sold.

"We hoped you would," said Mr. Kincaid. "Ms. Eberlin wanted me to be sure to tell you that you will get a complimentary square for your own family."

"That's sweet. My son would love that."

"Glad to hear it. I'll be in touch with further details."

They said goodbye, and Marissa hung up with her first real smile that day. Owen would love to decorate the chalk square with her. In fact, he'd probably spend days trying to figure out what to draw. When it came to keepsake items, her son was very serious. This would be a lot of fun.

Then she remembered the festival was on Jacob's property, and her smile fell.

Oh, yeah. Lots of fun.

This would be interesting. Jacob hesitated outside the door to Marissa's shop, hands shoved in the pockets of his fireman uniform, stalling as the afternoon sun warmed his neck around his polo collar. The last time he went inside Your Special Day, he'd ruined his developing relationship with Marissa. Had she forgiven him yet? Even now, her cold parting words echoed in his mind. *Make what work?* Ouch. Had she not felt the same connection he did? Surely she had—she'd agreed to go out with him, after all.

Not that it mattered anymore.

Jacob jingled his truck keys in his pocket, trying to decide if he should knock, go inside or forget it and head to work. He looked down at his shirt and sighed. It was possibly a mistake to wear his uniform in front of Marissa, as it would only serve as a harsh reminder of their confrontation Monday. But he was scheduled to be at the station in an hour, and besides, this was who he was—he didn't have any reason to apologize for that.

So why did he feel so guilty?

Jacob opened the door, wincing at the harsh jangle of the bell announcing his presence. It might as well have been a siren, given how fast Marissa jumped from her seated position behind the desk. She stood, but didn't say a word. Just stared at him as if shocked he'd dared to show up.

Actually, he was still a little surprised himself.

Jacob cleared his throat. "I, uh—I got the cacti." The words sounded even stupider leaving his mouth than they did in his head. *Smooth move.* He should have gone to work as his instincts warned.

Marissa's eyebrows rose as she silently waited for further explanation.

"The cacti. From the nursery on the Boardwalk. Remember?"

She inclined her chin in acknowledgment, crossing her arms over her suit jacket. "I remember."

Finally, she spoke—even if her voice did sound tight enough to snap in two. Jacob halfway expected her to ask him to leave. He waited by the door a heartbeat. Maybe he should spare her the request—spare both of them—and go. He put one hand on the knob. But something lurking beneath the hardened glaze in her eyes made him think twice. Jacob hesitated, and then crossed the room in a few easy strides. "Marissa, I'd really like for us to be okay."

Her eyes widened at his bold proclamation, and she stepped backward a half step, even though the desk still separated them. "What do you mean?"

"I know you're still upset with me, and I can see how awful this whole situation looks. But I promise you, I didn't lie to you about your son."

"I know." To Jacob's surprise, Marissa sank into her chair and propped her chin on her elbows, as if tired of holding her own weight. "I know."

"Then can you forgive me?"

"I already did." She sighed, pushing her hair back from her face before meeting his gaze.

The vulnerability tore at his emotions, and he sat slowly on the chair across from her. "Then what's wrong?"

"I'm…disappointed."

Hope jerked for attention in Jacob's heart. Maybe Marissa didn't mean what she said at their last parting, after all. But what good was it for her to feel the same way about him if they couldn't do anything about it? The fledging hope faded, leaving a bitter aftertaste. Jacob reached for her hand across the desk before he could think better of it, and gave it a soft squeeze. "So am I."

Their gazes locked and held, and something stirred inside Jacob that hadn't in a long time. Not with any of the women he'd dated recently—or ever, for that matter. This was different. Deeper. More than a physical spark, though there was certainly that.

He studied the depths of her eyes, void of their usual life. How could he push her away? But how could he risk losing his job and not being able to take care of his brother and his family? He'd cut Ryan a check just last week to help cover grocery money. If Jacob upset the chief—any more than he already had with the water hose incident—by coming on to his daughter, how could he provide for his loved ones? He still felt responsible for

Ryan's situation. He'd encouraged his brother into a career path that dead-ended. Whether that was his fault or not, Ryan was his little bro. Jacob was just as responsible for him now as he was when they were growing up.

Jacob slowly brought his hand away from Marissa's, his skin immediately missing the contact. Marissa clasped her hands together, as if suddenly unsure what to do with them. Jacob swallowed hard. "We're going to be working together on this festival and for Olivia's party. Can we start over?" He wished in the way they both wanted to, but that was impossible. They needed a fresh start—as coworkers and friends, nothing more. He smiled hesitantly. "I know that's a lot to ask."

Marissa's lips straightened into a thin line. "You don't understand how much."

"Enlighten me." He wanted to understand, wanted to fix this. There had to be something else going on with her besides the discovery of his true career. Why could it possibly matter so much, especially if she finally understood that he hadn't lied to her?

Marissa briefly closed her eyes. When she opened them, the startling emerald color, glossy with emotion, nearly knocked him from his chair. He clenched one hand into a fist to keep from taking her hand in his again.

When she spoke, her words were leveled, controlled, as if she were making extreme effort to keep her emotions at bay. "I don't like people influencing my son without my knowing about it. When I realized you were the fireman that Owen was so excited about from school, I snapped. I don't want Owen to be a fireman when he grows up." The dam broke and tears clogged her words. Marissa stared at her desk instead of at Jacob, jaw clenched. "I overreacted. But this is a hot-button issue with me right now, and well—it was a lot at once."

"No, I'm the one who's sorry." Jacob shifted positions in his chair, feeling like a heel. No wonder she'd reacted as she did. It seemed pretty premature for her to be worried about Owen's career path, but he wasn't a mom. He had no right to judge. Jacob let out a slow breath. "I had no idea it was such a big deal for you." He knew she had personal issues with her father, but enough for her to practically hate the entire career? A flood of sympathy washed over him.

"You couldn't have." She lifted one shoulder in a shrug. "I apologize for getting upset. That wasn't professional of me."

"Marissa…" Jacob's voice trailed off and he couldn't help it. He rounded the desk to stand closer to her, resting his weight against the tabletop, and took her hand. "I would hope we were past professional by now."

"We were. Are," she corrected. Marissa looked up at him, then at their hands touching, and slowly drew hers back into her lap. "But to what end?"

Not a good one. At least, not one either of them—it seemed—wanted. Jacob moved away from the desk to give her space, each inch separating them seeming like an ever-widening chasm. "I'm not sure." He couldn't make himself voice the hopelessness of their situation. Not again.

Not with the memory of her soft palm against his still embedded in his mind like a brand.

"Exactly." Marissa's eyes belied the same disappointment he felt all the way through to his gut. Then she straightened her shoulders, held out her hand in a formal handshake and smiled brightly. "Hi, I'm Marissa Hawthorne. I believe I'm planning your niece's princess-themed birthday party?"

Jacob couldn't help but grin back at her attempt to literally start over. If only it were that easy. He shook her hand, forcing the chemistry between them out of his thoughts. "Nice to meet you. I'm Jacob Greene—a fireman with a lawn service for a side job."

Marissa snorted back a laugh. "Good to know. So, what did you have in mind for your niece's party?" She gestured for him to take a seat once again, and he obeyed with mixed emotions. Part of him wanted to rush out the door and away from the reminder of what he couldn't have—and desperately wanted. Yet the other part of him could stay right there and stare happily at Marissa for the rest of the day.

Jacob sneaked a peek at his watch. He needed to be at work in less than half an hour. But as he listened to Marissa fill him in on what she'd planned for Olivia's party so far, and watched the way her eyes lit with excitement and her graceful hands gestured in animation, he figured he could spare a few more minutes.

At this point, he was great at putting off the inevitable.

Chapter Eight

"One incredibly heavy box of red, white and blue paraphernalia, at your service." Jacob hoisted a large cardboard box, fresh from the UPS van outside, onto Marissa's desk with ease.

"Oh, good, it came early." Marissa cut the packing tape with a pair of scissors and peered into the box containing hundreds of pinwheels, balloons, rolls of stickers, Slinky toys, and buttons, still warm from the delivery truck. "And nothing is bent up. Excellent."

"I think using a red, white and blue patriotic color scheme for the fundraiser was genius," Liz said as she joined her brother-in-law and Marissa at the desk. She plucked a pinwheel from the bubble wrapping and blew. The colored spokes spun happily.

"I hope so. I don't want people to think we're trying to pull off a Fourth of July celebration in

May." Marissa frowned. Maybe she should have stuck with something simpler, like a flower theme. Or pastels to represent spring.

Liz shook her head. "Firemen are heroes of our country, just like people in the military. Red, white and blue is the perfect reminder of that."

Jacob tapped the box with one finger. "Where do you want these? I'm assuming not on the middle of your desk for another two weeks." He grinned, and Marissa's stomach flipped as it had yesterday when Jacob spent most of the day with her and Liz, helping with fundraiser details and last-minute party plans. He'd done everything from printing princess-themed coloring pages from a website online to tying ribbons around individual goody bags for each party guest. Not to mention he fielded several phone calls about the fundraiser from master gardeners, and double-checked to make sure his lawn service employees were on schedule to finish prepping his yard for the festival next week. As much as Jacob's proximity reminded her of what she couldn't have, he—and his sister-in-law—had been a big help the past few days. Unfortunately, once Marissa's shock and anger about Jacob's secret faded, she'd had nothing left to protect her heart from falling even harder.

Jacob stared at her, waiting for an answer, and Marissa quickly shook her head. "Sorry. Lots to think about." She avoided his questioning eyes, hoping he wouldn't assume the truth—that she was thinking about him. But she felt his steady gaze on her face as she looked at the box of pinwheels. "We can store these in the back room, wherever there's space. This close to the festival, it's going to be a madhouse around here."

"As you wish." Jacob toted the box down the short hall to the storage room at the back of the shop.

Liz turned to Marissa, her hands clasped in front of her. "I can't tell you how excited Olivia is about her party next Saturday. She keeps practicing a curtsy in front of my full-length mirror. I keep telling her it's still a week away, but you know kids."

"I'm glad." Marissa hoped Liz hadn't noticed her watching Jacob walk away. She tried to focus. "I think everything is almost set for her big day."

"And I'll be on my days off from the station, so I'll be there to help." Jacob returned, dusting his hands on his jeans.

Great. She meant that both sarcastically and sincerely, if that were possible. She enjoyed his company, but that was becoming the problem. They were together too much for her to guard her heart. Marissa couldn't keep up with Jacob's fire department schedule, and, she had to admit to herself, she hadn't wanted to try. She'd accepted that if Jacob was off duty, he was helping her and Liz in the shop with the parties. If he didn't show up, then he was working—at the little brick station that separated them like the Atlantic separated America from Europe. But, Olivia would be glad her beloved uncle was at her party, and that was the bottom line. It was Olivia's day, not Marissa's, so she'd do like she'd done all week since her and Jacob's truce—fake it 'til she meant it.

"Busy day." Jacob pulled one arm to his side in a stretch, and then checked his watch. "I'm starved."

"You're always starved." Liz swatted Jacob's arm. "Some things never change. You and Ryan are so much alike."

"I'll take that as a compliment." Jacob winked. "Who wants lunch from the diner down the block? My treat." He grabbed his truck keys from his pocket and jangled them in front of the girls like bait. "I'll even spring for Tater Tots."

"Count me in." Liz grabbed a notepad from Marissa's desk and jotted down her order. "What do you want, Marissa?"

"Cheeseburger and Tater Tots are fine. Mustard only on the burger." She'd usually go for a salad, but she'd worked up an appetite today—physically and emotionally. Comfort food sounded good.

"Got it." Liz slapped the list against Jacob's broad chest and Marissa couldn't help but wish she had the same right to tease and joke around with him.

Just not as a sister.

Cheeks flushed, she turned to her desk and grabbed the nearest file on top, pretending to peruse the contents as if they were of the utmost importance. She kept her head down until the shop door closed behind Jacob, and then looked up as Liz plopped down in front of her.

"Girl, what gives?"

She feigned innocence. "What do you mean?"

"I know you and Jacob worked out the argument you had earlier in the week about his career and Owen." Liz crossed her legs, then paused to brush at a piece of lint on her knee. "I didn't realize you were falling for him."

"I'm not falling for him." The lie burned Marissa's lips and she swallowed, staring at the thread still clinging to Liz's pant leg instead of meeting her new friend's eyes. "I mean, I'm not trying to. It's irrelevant, regardless."

"How so?"

"I think he feels that he can't get involved with me because my father is his boss. He's afraid it would mess things up for him at work. And I can't get involved with him because no matter how much I care for Jacob—"

"So you admit it." Liz sat back with a smug grin.

Marissa continued as if she hadn't been interrupted, ignoring the flush heating her neck. "I can't be in a relationship with a fireman. It's that simple."

Liz frowned. "Maybe I'm missing a step. That doesn't seem very simple at all."

"You don't understand." Marissa stood abruptly and grabbed another box from the floor by her chair. "Come on, we still need to distribute these posters advertising the festival. Let's see if we can hang a few around the neighborhood before Jacob gets back."

"I'm a mom, too, remember," Liz warned as she accepted the roll of tape Marissa handed her. "I know a dodge when I see one. But you're not a kid, so I'll let it go." She touched Marissa's arm and waited until Marissa looked at her, her voice softening. "Please know I'm here if you need to talk, okay? Parenting is hard enough with two parents, much less alone. It brings a lot of stress that carries over into other areas of our lives. It's okay to get overwhelmed—just don't let it control your life, okay?"

"That's not it." Marissa hesitated at the door, balancing the box of flyers on her hip. She stared at the silver knob under her hand, the metal cool against her palm. A question teased her lips, begging for release. She hesitated, then plunged. "Do you ever feel relieved that Ryan was let go?"

Liz's eyebrows shot to her hairline and down

again. "No, can't say that I do." She laughed. "Shockingly enough, I enjoyed regular paychecks and insurance."

"I meant now that he's not a fireman anymore, he's safe." The statement sounded a little ridiculous even to her own ears, and Marissa wished she could take the question back. But she had to know. Wouldn't she feel that way, if Kevin were still around and was let go? How many times had she begged him to change careers over the course of their marriage?

Liz drew in her bottom lip, understanding dawning in her hazel eyes. "I supported my husband in his career. Happily." She shrugged. "I figure God has it under control. He'll either keep Ryan safe, or He'll have a good reason not to. That's not up to me."

"How can you say that so lightly?" The words whispered from Marissa's lips and she gripped the knob tighter, trying to hold back a sudden onslaught of tears. God hadn't protected Kevin, and she couldn't ever begin to imagine how she could feel okay with that fact. Even if her love for Kevin had faded, even if the memories of their rocky attempt at marriage had dimmed, how could she accept the fact that God was in control and that was that?

"I don't say it lightly," Liz answered. She took the heavy box from Marissa's arm, and offered a sympathetic smile. "Sometimes you have to let Someone else carry the burden."

Marissa felt useless without something to hold, and she quickly took the box back. "I get your point. Thanks."

Liz opened the door and ushered Marissa through. "You should come to church with us this Sunday. I really think Owen would love our kids' ministry."

Church. Marissa closed the door behind them, stalling. Sunshine greeted her with a rush of warmth and she tilted her face to the blue sky above, wishing her fears could thaw as quickly as her skin. She hadn't gone to a church service in years, but Liz was right—Owen would like it. He deserved a chance to grow up in Sunday school as Marissa had. But was it wrong to sit on the pew when her heart felt the way it did about God's sovereignty? She chewed on her bottom lip as Liz waited patiently for an answer.

Finally, Marissa nodded. "Okay. We'll give it a try." For Owen's sake. She hoisted the box to her other hip as they began their trek to the streetlight post by the curb, feeling its weight grow heavier with every step.

"What's Sunday school?" Owen's brow furrowed and his grip on his toy fire truck tightened. "I already go to school, Mom. I don't want to go on the weekends, too." Panic laced his voice from his position on the living room floor, and he sat back on his heels to look up at Marissa.

Guilt pricked Marissa's heart. Owen had gone to church with her many times as a toddler, but that was back when he went to the nursery room and she went to the service alone. Obviously he would have no recollection. "This isn't like your real school, buddy. It's church. You'll get to learn a story from the Bible and do an art project and play with other kids."

Owen's smile returned and he began pushing his truck on the floor. "That sounds cool. Why haven't we been before?"

"We used to go, before—" Marissa swallowed the rest of her sentence, not wanting to put either of them in a bad mood. *Before your dad died.* "Come on, buddy, it's time for bed. Pj's and teeth." She watched to make sure Owen brushed all of his teeth and not just the front ones, then tucked him into bed, grateful he hadn't inquired further about their lack of church attendance. She felt guilty enough already. "Sweet dreams." She kissed his forehead.

"Night, Mom." Owen burrowed in his pillow, his red sheets pulled up to his ear. Then he popped upright. "Wait, I forgot my fire truck."

Marissa's stomach tightened, wishing the symbol of the truck didn't mean so much to him—and wishing that it didn't bother her so badly that it did. "It's in the living room. You can get it tomorrow." She couldn't fight that battle tonight. Not again.

"Mom—"

"Owen, it's late. No toys in bed."

He sighed, but didn't protest as he nestled back against the sheets. Marissa turned on his nightlight with a soft click, then shut his door halfway before collapsing in the living room chair with a sigh. She clicked on the late-night news, eager for a distraction from long-buried thoughts of Kevin, the fire department and church.

No such luck. On the screen, flames licked the roof of a ten-story office complex in downtown Orchid Hill above a red banner announcing BREAKING NEWS. Marissa's fingers clenched the remote control as the familiar adrenaline rush flooded her system. Even after Kevin had passed away, the panic remained automatic at seeing flames. She inhaled deeply, trying to distance herself from the report on the screen. Kevin was gone. Her dad didn't work the front lines. She had no reason to be concerned for anyone's safety anymore.

Jacob.

Her heart constricted, then thudded twice like a drumbeat. Was Jacob working this fire? Was he on duty tonight? She sat up in the recliner, her pulse pounding so loudly the sensation fairly vibrated her skin. She should have kept up with his schedule better. But it didn't matter.

Did it?

She stared at the scene unfolding before her on the television. The news anchor's voice seemed far away as Marissa watched the smoke unfurl from the windows of the top floor, anxiety raking across her back like fingernails. "Suspected electrical fire at the east 4400 block of downtown Orchid Hill," the brunette woman said on the screen, her expression tight. "Firefighters are currently working the scene. Thankfully no one was in the building at the time of the fire." The feed cut to a group of firemen, identical in their yellow bunker gear, holding streaming hoses toward the blaze. Police tried to keep concerned onlookers on the curb across the street and out of the way. Rubberneckers, Kevin used to call them—neighbors and pedestrians who caused more accidents by attempting to sate their curiosity instead of staying clear of the scene.

The phone rang. Marissa jerked, dropping the remote on her bare toes. She clenched her eyes against the stab of pain and grabbed the cordless from the receiver on the end table. She gritted her teeth. "Hello?"

"Are you watching the news?"

Marissa's eyes flew open at her father's voice,

as all remnants of pain from her foot disappeared. He hadn't called in, what, a month? Two months? "Yes. Are you downtown?" Chaos reigned in the background, and she wondered why she even asked. Of course her dad would be there. He might not be able to be counted on for family matters, but his accountability to his work went beyond predictable.

"Yeah, I'm here. It's under control, almost out. I figured you'd be watching." He cleared his throat, and Marissa frowned. The chief rarely called her during—or even after—fires, even the big emergencies. Had the scene made him emotional? She scoffed. Surely not. This was Chief Brady, after all. But a small piece of Marissa's heart wanted it to be true. She pressed her lips together, waiting, unsure what to say to encourage an admission or—dare she hope—affection.

"This is exactly why I didn't want you to get involved with the community fundraiser."

Her hopes fell at his harsh tone, shattering into multiple shards near her bruised toe. Figured. Her dad had about as many emotions as Owen had stain-free T-shirts. She sighed. "Dad, I—"

"I'm serious, Marissa. This is above your head. We've gotten email threats and had vandalism at several stations. You can't tell me it's unrelated to the layoffs." A siren punctuated his sentence and he waited until it passed, then lowered his voice. "This was an arson fire."

"What? The news anchor said electrical." Arson? Not in Orchid Hill—impossible. Orchid Hill was considered by many magazines to be "the biggest little small town in the Deep South." That kind of crime just didn't happen.

The chief snorted. "The media reports what we tell them—at least at first. Technically, it was electrical."

Marissa frowned. "Then what's the problem?"

"It was electrical, as in someone broke inside the office complex to the main, cut the electrical wires and created sparks—then helped things along with gasoline."

Oh. Still, that didn't prove a connection to the layoffs. He was being paranoid. "Dad, the community isn't holding a grudge. Everyone wants to help, hence the whole point of the fundraiser." She bit her lip to keep from adding what she really wanted to say—that her dad could have possibly saved those men's jobs if he'd been willing to risk negative publicity and fight for them.

"I don't think it's that simple. People do crazy things for revenge and no one knows how to start a fire better than a fireman." A hiss, probably steam from the hoses, sounded over the line, followed by the slamming of what was likely a car door. "Listen, I need to go. I only wanted to tell you to quit this fundraiser nonsense and think logically."

She balked. "Tell me?"

The chief coughed. "All right, all right—*ask* you to reconsider your involvement with the fundraiser. I'd rather you stay out of the media altogether. We don't want any criminals getting ideas."

The word *ask* had likely lodged in his throat a few times before emerging. Marissa would have laughed if the entire situation wasn't so unbelievably frustrating. She clenched the phone in a tight grip and shook her head. "It's too late. Things are already in the works." An image of Jacob teased the fringes of her mind and she swallowed. *More than you know.* "Besides, I'm still not convinced this fire is connected anyway. You're jaded."

"And you're naive." He muttered something that might have been a goodbye before the line clicked into silence.

Marissa returned the phone to its receiver, wishing she'd been able to ask about Jacob's involvement with the fire tonight. But her father would have said something if any of his men had been injured—and so would the news anchor.

The chief's words replayed in Marissa's head as she watched the flames slowly extinguish on the television. *The media reports what we tell them.*

She turned the TV off with a click and made her way through the dark living room to her bedroom. Her dad didn't have the right to be overprotective anymore. He gave that up with every missed party, late dinner and skipped school play. Besides, she knew the people of Orchid Hill. No one would react to the layoffs in such a drastic manner. Her father was mistaken.

About a lot of things.

Chapter Nine

Jacob had never seen anyone so beautiful look so nervous. He watched Marissa clutch a Bible in her left hand, her right hand absently working the purple jeweled charm on the end of her necklace as she looked down at Owen. "You sure you'll be okay, buddy?" Her purple silky dress, cinched in the middle with a black belt, set off the blond in her hair and the green in her eyes until Jacob could hardly bear to look away.

Owen frowned up at his mom, as if he couldn't imagine why she'd even ask such a thing. "Uh, yeah, Mom. You said this would be fun, didn't you? Not like real school."

Marissa smiled, but the motion was almost lost beneath the worry in her eyes. "You're right. It will be fun." She looked away, biting her lower lip, and Jacob frowned. There was no way she was this worked up over her son going to a Sunday

school class. No, there was something else causing the bags beneath her eyes and the lines in her
brow and he didn't think it had anything to do
with the stress over Olivia's upcoming party or
the fundraiser.

More likely it had everything to do with the
panicked glances she kept casting around them as
if the church might literally bite her if she stayed
a moment longer.

"It'll be great." Jacob shifted his weight, not
used to standing in one place for so long in his
dress shoes that squashed his toes—and also not
fooled by Marissa's fake smile. He wished he
could hug her. But that would be overstepping
the defined line drawn in the proverbial sand. He
cleared his throat, leaning closer and lowering his
voice to avoid drawing Owen's attention. "Are you
okay?"

Marissa nodded, meeting his eyes briefly before
glancing back at her son. "I'm fine."

He opened his mouth to protest, but Olivia
interrupted. "Our teacher is nice," she assured
Owen, looking sweet as always in a floral-print
dress and pink shoes. "I think this week we're
going to learn about Noah. He's the guy who built
a really big boat."

"Awesome. Boats are almost as cool as fire
trucks." Owen beamed with excitement, and Jacob
caught the wince Marissa stifled a moment too

late. He quickly checked his watch. The service was about to start, and not a minute too soon. He still didn't understand Marissa's aversion to firefighting, but he could save them from this moment, if nothing else. He hunched down, not caring if he wrinkled his carefully ironed pants, and reached out to Owen. "Want me to walk you to your class, buddy? We better hurry—it's almost time for it to start." He felt Marissa's sharp gaze stab the side of his face at the unintentional use of her son's nickname, and his heart sank like a rock to the pit of his stomach. *Uh-oh.*

Thankfully, Liz took over before he could cause another blunder—or before Owen could eagerly take him up on his apparently inappropriate offer. Liz gently touched Owen's shoulder, steering him with Olivia toward the double doors at the end of the church foyer. "Olivia will show you where to go, Owen. We'll see you after the service, okay?"

"Okay. Bye, Mom!" Owen waved cheerfully to Marissa before turning and running with Olivia toward their room. He made race car noises and they laughed as they skidded around the corner, Olivia's pink hair ribbon trailing behind them.

"That was easy." Liz laughed, but Marissa still looked more upset than amused. The rock wedged in Jacob's stomach and refused to budge. He shouldn't have been so careless, stepping in like that. He didn't have the right. But he could tell by the way Owen had remained stuck like glue to his side during the school presentation and this morning that he trusted him, looked up to him—even before Jacob knew the connection with Marissa. How could he blow that off?

"Come on. We'd better go find Ryan." Jacob gestured for the ladies to walk first, wishing he could put his hand on Marissa's back to guide her as they went. He opened the sanctuary doors and they filed into the pew near the middle that Ryan had saved for them.

"Sit by me, Marissa." Liz settled into the seat by her husband and motioned for Marissa to slide in next. She dutifully followed, and Jacob sat on the end, hoping he hadn't landed too close—though he would likely feel her presence even from an entirely different row. Liz made quick introductions between Ryan and Marissa, and they shook hands as the organist played a rousing chorus.

Jacob glanced at Marissa. But she still wasn't looking at him. Should he apologize for the endearment he'd used toward Owen or let it go? He debated, but the music minister requested the congregation rise before he could decide.

Marissa stood beside Jacob as he opened the thick hymnal, the lilac scent of her hair distracting him from the words on the page. He sung the lines about grace and redemption, stealing glances at Marissa from the corner of his eye. Her expression still waxed pale and she clenched the pew in front of her with white knuckles as she sang softly along.

Man, he wanted more Sundays like this. Preferably without her being angry at him, of course, but with time maybe her dislike of the fire department would cease and therefore her overprotection of Owen as well.

But that still didn't change the fact that Marissa was the chief's daughter—a truth that was slowly becoming less and less relevant the longer he breathed in the sweet smell of her hair. Maybe some things were worth the risk.

From down the pew, Ryan's rich baritone filled the air with the closing chorus, and Jacob's hopes crashed with reality. His little brother sang as wholeheartedly as he did everything else in his life—his family, his work, his faith. Ryan trusted that God would provide for his family despite their dismal financial circumstances, and right now that provision was funneling straight through Jacob.

Leaving no room for a lilac-scented distraction.

She didn't belong here. Not in the pew, surrounded by people openly living their faith, not in church, where she'd barely set foot for the past five years—and certainly not beside Jacob, the scent of his spicy cologne making her wish she could rewrite the last several days of history and start over. Really start over—not just with the tentative truce they'd formed, but further back than that, when he'd first strolled into her life across the parking lot of Your Special Day. Maybe if she'd guarded her heart and remained professional instead of allowing herself the long-buried joy of flirting, of feeling attractive and like a woman instead of a mother, she could have avoided the ache that came with sitting so close to Jacob—yet remaining so painfully far away.

Marissa stared at the preacher standing in the pulpit, his booming voice causing congregation members to nod in agreement or voice hushed *amens* as the truths of the sermon pierced their hearts. She used to be one of them, sitting on the second or third row at her old church, soaking in God's word and making excuses for her husband's absence, knowing full well that if Kevin wasn't at the station he likely wouldn't have been on the bench beside her anyway. Kevin had considered religion more of a crutch than a real way of living, a way to fellowship with God. Despite his showing interest in faith when they'd dated, he changed his mind after they married.

Like he'd done with a lot of things.

Jacob shifted on the pew beside Marissa, his leg nearly grazing hers in the cramped space, and she stared at his hands clutching a well-worn, dog-eared copy of the Bible. She could feel his presence next to her as tangibly as if they were touching, and she quickly looked back at the pulpit as Jacob's gaze drifted sideways toward her. Did he feel the connection, too? Judging from his sidelong glances, he might. But it didn't matter. Couldn't.

God, why does the perfect man have to embody all of my worst fears? The prayer slipped easily from her mind toward the high ceiling of the church, and for the first time in a while, seemed as if it didn't merely bounce off the wooden structure but made its way to the heavens. *Are You still listening?* Not that she deserved to have her prayers answered. She'd turned away from God after Kevin's death—making her as guilty as Kevin for turning away while he was still alive.

She studied Jacob's profile as he listened to the pastor. His dark hair grazing his collar, his strong jaw boasting just a hint of shadow. He wasn't really perfect. After all, he'd hurt her feelings in the first week they'd met and continually upset her with his closeness to her son. No one was truly perfect. But a man who loved his family, spoiled his niece, helped a stranger with a flat tire and obviously spent time with his creased leather Bible sure did come pretty close.

Yet even if Jacob felt the freedom to risk his career for her—and it would be a risk, she knew her father well—he was still a man who would ultimately put his career first. It was the nature of the job, as the chief and Kevin had proven over and over. Jacob would still be on call, working long hours, missing family events and scaring her with every missed phone call. As different as Kevin and Jacob appeared to be, nothing would be different at all as long as he was a fireman.

A chuckle from the congregation wrenched Marissa from the shackles of the past and the shadows of the future, and guilt spread through her stomach. The sermon was wrapping up and she'd not comprehended a single word. She stood numbly beside Jacob as the organ offered a coaxing melody down the aisle. The familiar words of the hymn burned her mind, filling her eyes with tears. She had never felt more unsteady in her life. Emotionally, physically, mentally. The room started to spin and she automatically touched Jacob's shoulder to balance herself.

"Are you okay?" His rich, warm voice filled her insides with longing and regret. No, she wasn't okay—and she wouldn't be as long as she kept reminding herself of everything she'd lost and could never have again. With God. With her faith.

With Jacob.

Marissa's hand fell to her side as the room straightened, and she forced a smile and nod to reassure him. His eyes remained locked on hers as the organ released the final chords of the music, urging people to come forward.

But her feet remained rooted in place.

The congregation filed out of the sanctuary, a steady stream of voices greeting each other, making plans to get together and debating lunch options. Jacob pressed as close to Marissa as he dared and bent down toward her ear. "Are you sure you're all right?" He hated to pester her— she'd already said yes twice—but she'd looked so little and lost, standing there in the row at church, clutching his shirtsleeve between her fingers and swaying slightly in place. She didn't look much better now, but at least the color had returned to her face and she seemed somewhat steadier.

Marissa smiled, but it didn't quite reach her eyes. "I'm fine. Like I said, I think my blood sugar dropped a little. I probably need to eat lunch." Her eyes scanned the passing crowd from their vantage point against the far wall of the lobby, probably searching for her son. Liz had braved the crowd to get the kids from their class, and Ryan stood a few feet away giving a deacon of the church an update about his job situation.

"Maybe we can all go get something to eat together." Jacob forced a happy note into his voice. Hopefully there'd be room for a cheeseburger with all the guilt he still felt rumbling around his stom-

ach every time Ryan explained his financial situation to a caring church member. Even though
Ryan didn't blame him and Jacob knew he hadn't
forced his little brother into the career, he still felt
responsible. No one else seemed to understand
the tie between big bro and little bro, especially
when Jacob had spent a good part of his teen years
taking care of Ryan while their single mother
worked two jobs to get by. "My treat, of course."

Marissa turned toward him then, and he nearly
took a step back at the pain in her sage green eyes.
"Why are you doing this?"

He held up both hands in defense. "Hey, it's
only lunch. If you'd rather wait and let me buy
dinner instead, that works, too."

The humor zipped straight over Marissa's head.
Her mouth formed a thin, straight line and her
eyes narrowed slightly. Jacob lowered his hands
with a sigh. "I'm kidding."

"I see that." Still no smile.

"Why am I doing what? I don't get it."

"That's the problem." She shook her head, her
hair brushing against the shoulders of her dress.
The golden strands against the purple fabric reminded him of royalty, and his own words from
the party supply store at the Boardwalk danced in
his mind's eye. *Every girl deserves to be a princess for a day.* Marissa's abrupt change of subject
in the store that night and the current exhaus-

tion in her eyes and tired slump of her shoulders proved she still didn't believe him.

"You're too nice to me." The words fell off her lips as she stood, staring into the crowd once again, her arms crossed defensively across her chest. "We don't need charity, and neither does your brother."

"It's not charity to offer to take my family out to lunch." Jacob's defenses rose and he crossed his own arms, mirroring her posture. What did she know about his family or his intentions? That wasn't fair.

"I'm not your family." She leveled her gaze on him in a pointed expression. "And neither is Owen."

He stared down at his shiny dress shoes, nodding a few times and gathering his composure before speaking. "I'm sorry I used your nickname for Owen earlier this morning, and offered to walk him to class. That obviously crossed a line."

"I'm really careful about Owen getting to know the men in my life. I have to protect him."

Men? Plural? Jacob winced. The thought burned his gut and he drew a deep breath. "I'm sure that's tough, and again, I'm sorry. It wasn't intentional. We really clicked at his school the other day and—"

"Nothing is intentional with you, is it?"

Jacob's head jerked in surprise, but Marissa

wasn't done. "First you didn't intentionally mean to hide your job from me, and now you're unintentionally bonding with my son. When will you just own up to what you do, Kevin?"

Understanding dawned in Jacob's mind as horror flashed in Marissa's eyes. "I'm sorry. I didn't mean—that was a slip—my husband." She covered her mouth with both hands.

"It's okay." Without thinking, Jacob gathered Marissa into his arms and pressed her head against his chest. His heart rocked a beat that would surely make her deaf, but holding her felt like nothing else ever had. She fit perfectly in his embrace, and he didn't care if old Widow Township was frowning with disapproval over her specs across the lobby. Who knew how long it'd been since Marissa had a real hug from someone who cared? She deserved that—and so much more.

"It's been an...emotional morning," she whispered into his shirt. "I haven't been to church since Kevin died. I—it was harder than I thought."

She missed her husband. Understandable, yet at the same time, dismay tightened its grip on Jacob's heart and disappointment broke a sweat onto his hairline. It'd been how many years since Kevin's death? And she still grieved to this level? Maybe it was for the best Jacob couldn't start a relationship with Marissa. Even if he was somehow able to secure the chief's blessing, she obviously wasn't anywhere near ready for such a step.

Jacob didn't protest as she stepped out of his embrace, sniffing and dabbing her eyes with the cuff of her dress. Owen rounded the corner then, carrying a construction paper ark and his children's Bible, Liz and Olivia right behind him. "Hey, Mom! Look what we made! Noah is the coolest guy ever." He babbled on about the animals going two by two into the giant boat, thankfully not seeming to notice the redness in Marissa's eyes. She recovered well, sharing a big smile that seemed more genuine toward her son than it had toward Jacob all morning. Marissa listened as Owen carried on, then mouthed "thank you" to Jacob over the top of her son's head.

Jacob nodded, afraid to speak lest his own emotion overtake him. But Liz caught the exchange and frowned, her eyes darting between him and Marissa's turned back as Marissa steered her son toward the parking lot—and a fast getaway. Jacob shook his head at his sister-in-law, not up for any matchmaking right now.

Maybe not ever.

Chapter Ten

The stapler slammed against the stack of invoices with more force than necessary. *Bam!* Marissa felt so stupid, accidentally calling Jacob by her husband's name yesterday at church. *Bam!* How ridiculous and overemotional could she be? She'd totally overreacted, but Jacob reminding her of his bonding with Owen at school had set her off like a time bomb. *Bam!* Jacob probably thought that she'd had this rotten, awful marriage, spouting her pent-up anger at Jacob in Kevin's stead. And well, some parts had been pretty awful, but not all of it. Besides, that was hardly the impression she wanted to leave on the man she was growing more attracted to despite every effort toward the opposite.

Marissa straightened the stapled invoices on her desk into tidy piles, hating that they blurred beneath her teary eyes. She blinked rapidly to clear them. When did her life become so dramatic? She'd been lying low, focusing on her job and Owen for the majority of the last five years, and had been doing fine. Lonely, maybe—but fine. Yet she'd cried more in the past week than she had since Kevin's funeral.

It changed when you met Jacob, a small voice prompted her conscience.

Marissa gritted her teeth. She wished she had something else to staple to drown out the voice of truth. The tinkling bell sounded suddenly from the front door, and she gratefully waved the delivery man inside. Even if this package came with a bill, it'd be a welcome distraction.

"Delivery for Ms. Hawthorne?" The delivery man walked inside carrying a vase overflowing with deep pink orchids, the arrangement concealing half his face and driving cap. He peered around the bouquet with a smile.

"That's me." She cleared a spot on her desk, heart pounding at the beautiful arrangement. "You can set them here." She watched as the elderly man gingerly set the giant vase on her desk. Who would send her flowers? Surely not her parents— it wasn't even her birthday. In fact, she hadn't received anything of this sort since her second year of marriage, when Kevin realized at the last minute that he'd better do *something* for Valentine's Day.

The man stepped back, pointing to the card tucked on a stand inside the potted dirt. "There's the note. Have a good day, ma'am." He winked. "Though I guess it's nice enough now, huh?"

Marissa smiled, wondering if it'd be rude to snatch the card and rip it open while he was still standing there. "We'll see." She waited until he headed back to his truck outside, then grabbed the white sealed packet. Her hands shook as she pulled the card from the mini-envelope.

Marissa,
I thought I'd send a formal apology for over-stepping my bounds yesterday with your son. I happen to think Owen is very special. It's hard not to treat him that way.
P.S. I think you are, too.
Sincerely, Jacob

Marissa closed her eyes, the printed words still visible in her mind. A formal apology. She snorted. She was the one who owed Jacob an apology. What kind of man said he was sorry in person and sent a beautiful flower bouquet the next day? A good man.

She dropped the card in the top drawer of her desk, wishing she could go home and press it, along with a petal from the arrangement, between the pages of her favorite book of poetry. But such antics would lead only to more heartache. Jacob was off-limits in so many ways, she didn't even know where to start.

The phone trilled on her desk, and she scooped it up, hoping it wasn't Jacob. What would she say? Apologize for her meltdown at the church? Thank him for the flowers? Too bad she couldn't click her shiny red heels like one of the characters in Owen's favorite movie and wish herself someplace far away. "Your Special Day, this is Marissa."

To her relief, Liz's perky voice filled the line. "Hey, girl. Busy day?"

Marissa glanced at the flowers on her desk, then at the stacks surrounding them. "No more than usual."

"What's the countdown for the festival now?"

Her gaze automatically drifted to the open calendar, not that she needed to double-check to know. "One week and four days."

"We'll be ready." Liz's statement sounded more like a question.

"We have to be." Marissa chuckled, but like everything lately, it felt forced. She cleared her throat to try to hide the dismal tone. "What's up?"

"I was calling to see if you and Owen would like to come over for dinner tomorrow night. I'm cooking up a big pot of gumbo and we need help eating it. Sound good?"

"Sounds great." Marissa smiled and this time, felt the motion sincerely through and through. As hectic as her schedule was right now between the birthday party and the festival, the surprise of Liz's friendship made it all worth it. She hadn't had a girlfriend in a long time—someone to chat with over the phone, stress with at work and trust with her tragic past. She'd ended up confiding in Liz at work the other day about Kevin having been a fireman, and Liz's sympathy and understanding had helped heal a crack in Marissa's fragile emotions, bonding them closer together. "What time?"

"Be here at six. I'll be the one with the chef's hat!"

"We'll be there." Marissa said goodbye and hung up, then made a notation in her daybook. Her pen caught the low-hanging leaves of the orchid arrangement in the vase and she quickly flicked the tip of the pen free, wishing it was as easy to untangle Jacob from her thoughts. *I happen to think Owen is very special...I think you are, too.*

"I can't believe you didn't tell me she was coming." Jacob tried to keep his voice down in Liz's kitchen, his grip on the wooden spoon tighter than necessary as he stirred the gumbo in the stockpot. He'd been expecting a nice, home-made meal with his family, and instead walked into the house to find Marissa sitting on the ottoman with her son and his niece, playing one of Olivia's handheld computer games and looking way too much like she belonged there.

Liz worked a red mitt over her hand and opened the oven door. "Well, I can't believe you sent her flowers and didn't tell *me*." The steaming bread she pulled from the warm rack filled the kitchen with the tangy scent of garlic and butter. Jacob's stomach growled, but he wouldn't let his meddling sister-in-law off the hook that easily.

"That was different. This is flat-out match-making." He jammed the lid on the pot and set the spoon on the counter with a clatter. The spicy aroma of sausage and shrimp wafted through the air. He wanted to lick the spoon but didn't think that would help give his end of the argument much merit.

Liz shut the oven with a smirk as she deposited the bread onto the cooktop. "And sending flowers isn't a sign of courting?"

"Courting!" Jacob forgot to lower his voice this time. He planted his hands on his hips. "First of all, this isn't the eighteenth century, and secondly, that's not the case."

"Only because you're both stubborn." Liz handed him a stack of dishes. "Could you set the table?"

He narrowed his eyes. "You're changing the subject."

"Maybe, but you're denying the inevitable."

"Uh, guys?" Ryan popped his head into the open doorway of the kitchen, his voice barely above a whisper. "Marissa does have ears, you know. Owen and Olivia are only drowning out so much of this conversation with their debate on which color fruit snack tastes better. Red is winning, if anyone cares."

"Sorry." Jacob's ears burned with as much frustration as embarrassment. He shouldn't have sent the flowers, knew they'd give the wrong impression, but he wanted to do something to make Marissa smile again. Wanted to replace the hurt he'd put in her eyes with something warm and light. She deserved that much. He hesitated, unsure how much to reveal. "Listen, Liz, I appreciate your train of thought here, but it's not going to happen with Marissa and me. It can't." *She's still grieving her ex.* The fact that Jacob had realized that while holding her in his arms inside the church was a cruel twist of the knife.

"I think it can." Liz turned the burner off on the

stove and shoved a pile of napkins on top of the plates Jacob still held.

"That's not your decision." Or even his, unfortunately. These matchmaking ways of Liz's only made the facts hurt that much more. He never would have predicted Marissa would tell Liz about the orchids and he'd spend the rest of the evening justifying his reasons for sending them.

Reasons he still couldn't fully justify even to himself.

"I'm going to set the table." Jacob turned his back on Liz's knowing grin and strode toward the dining room. He was grateful he had a family that cared enough to meddle, but wouldn't it be enough to feed him from time to time and leave him to his bachelor ways? He knew Liz and Marissa becoming friends would be trouble, but he had no idea exactly how much—until now.

"This is going to be the longest dinner ever." He set the plates on the table, a little louder than necessary, and hastily crammed a napkin under each one. Too bad he'd have to eat and run. Staying in Marissa's presence longer than necessary would hurt worse than an upset stomach. He inhaled deeply. Man, that gumbo smelled better than anything he'd had in days—not that that was shocking, since Steve had been on kitchen duty again. He set the silverware on the table. As soon as they wolfed down dinner, he'd head out.

"The bread pudding's ready!" Liz called from the kitchen.

Jacob's stomach flipped in protest. Okay, so maybe he'd stay for dessert. But no longer.

"Mom, Ms. Liz's gumbo is better than yours. Can you get the recipe?" Owen's spoon clattered into his empty bowl and Marissa looked up with a start.

Ryan snorted from across the table, then coughed loudly to cover it up. Beside Marissa, Jacob ducked his head, probably in an attempt to hide his own smile. At least they were trying to be polite. A twinge of embarrassment plucked at her, but she couldn't berate Owen for his honesty. Liz's gumbo *was* amazing. "Sure, Owen, that can be arranged." She wouldn't take it personally. At least he was eating well.

Marissa turned to Liz, who sat at the end of the table by Olivia. "You probably didn't expect a seven-year-old to eat half the pot."

"It's a compliment. I'm honored." Liz dabbed her mouth with a napkin as she stood. "And I'll get that recipe for you before you leave. Ryan, would you help me get the dessert, please?" Together they cleared the table, leaving Jacob and Marissa alone with the kids.

Owen and Olivia were now discussing their Sunday school class and what Bible story they might be learning next, jabbering excitedly and leaving Marissa no room for participation. She couldn't dodge talking directly to Jacob any longer. She'd avoided him most of the evening, which hadn't been hard since he'd hidden out in the kitchen with Liz before dinner. She could have sworn she heard her name come up in conversation several times, but figured she was being paranoid. Why would they be discussing her?

Although, Liz had forgotten to tell Marissa that Jacob would be at dinner when she invited her and Owen. Had she done so on purpose?

Marissa glanced Jacob's way, their elbows nearly touching on the worn tabletop, and quickly lowered her arm to her lap. Dinner had been nice, but borderline awkward. It almost seemed as if Jacob didn't want her there. But he'd sent the flowers, so that couldn't be the case. Still, something was a little off. Maybe he felt embarrassed about her slipup at church last Sunday. She knew she did.

"He's quite the character." Jacob's warm voice broke into her thoughts, and Marissa followed his gaze toward Owen. "I'm sure your gumbo is good, too."

"It's really not. But thanks." She smiled, wishing they could find the camaraderie they'd had before her blunder the other day. Her smile faded, and she met Jacob's eyes, forcing herself not to look away. "I never said thanks for the flowers. So, thanks. They were beautiful."

Jacob leaned back in his chair with a sigh. "You're welcome. And it's my fault. I never really gave you the chance to say anything." At the end of the table, Olivia giggled at the shadow puppet Owen was making against the dining room wall. He watched them with a slight smile. "I didn't mean to be so distant this evening. I'm a little frustrated with my sister-in-law, but that's not your fault."

Marissa frowned. "What did Liz do?"

"Did she tell you I would be here tonight?"

Marissa shook her head.

"She's matchmaking."

"Oh." Marissa swallowed. "I'm sorry, I—"

"Like I said, not your fault." Jacob's gaze collided with hers, and he reached over and squeezed her hand. "I just wish…" His voice trailed off and he abruptly shoved his chair back from the table. "Hey, guys, do you know how to do the goose puppet?" He moved to the end of the table by the kids and arranged Owen's hands into the proper form for the bird shadow.

Marissa watched with a lump in her throat. Why hadn't he finished his thought? Maybe he was as intimidated by the truth as she was. Because it didn't matter what he wished, or even what she wished. Jacob obviously didn't feel comfortable starting a relationship with her while under her father. And she couldn't—wouldn't—feel safe starting one with him as long as he was a fireman.

Jacob laughed then, the rich sound filling the dining room with warmth and a sweetness that settled in Marissa's heart like the brown sugar and cinnamon on top of Liz's bread pudding dessert. Who was she kidding? She and Jacob already had a relationship. It just remained locked in a box, starving for air and desperate to grow—but dying a slow death of denial.

Reality stung even more watching Jacob interact with her son. He was good with Owen, listening to his requests, taking his comments seriously, making him feel grown-up and important. Marissa cupped her hands under her chin and watched as Jacob taught both of the kids how to make various animals with their hands, complete with sound effects. He'd be a great father one day. She closed her eyes briefly, wishing away the thought. Even though Jacob showed amazing potential at being a dad, he was still a negative influence on Owen in regard to the one thing Marissa feared most. Owen already looked up to Jacob with near hero worship. Because of the lack of solid male role models in Owen's life, she wouldn't forbid their time together. But neither could she encourage it further by pursuing Jacob.

Liz and Ryan returned with the bread pudding and plates, their easy banter with each other carving a hole in Marissa's heart as they set the dessert on the table and passed out clean forks. Would she ever have that kind of teasing, fun love relationship? She and Kevin hadn't even had it for a long time after they married, but she could easily imagine it with Jacob. Memories of their easy interaction the first day they met in the parking lot at Your Special Day played in her mind like a movie as she spooned a bite of bread pudding into her mouth. Jacob's muscles under his shirt as he worked on her SUV's tire. The kindness in his eyes as he talked about his family and Olivia's party. The dimples that flashed every time he smiled—at her.

The sticky mixture in her dessert coated Marissa's tongue with a bittersweet flavor. She looked up as Jacob ruffled Owen's hair, his dimples in full bloom again as he chuckled at her son's attempt to do a dog puppet. That was Jacob. Mr. Considerate. Mr. Patient. Mr. Perfect. Marissa pushed her dessert dish away from her, suddenly full.

How could someone so perfect be so perfectly wrong for her?

Chapter Eleven

Jacob would say he couldn't eat or sleep, but he had, and did. He just didn't want to—because thoughts of Marissa on a full stomach sent him reaching for the antacids, and every time he laid down, he dreamed of her smile. To say he had it bad, as Liz would put it, was somewhat of an understatement. The more he tried to push Marissa out of his mind and heart, the more she burrowed in.

He rolled the push mower he used for maintaining smaller yards into the trailer, then slammed the mini-gate shut with a loud clank of metal. The hot noon sun burned his forearms and warmed the top of his baseball cap as he made his way to the truck cab, glad his employee had called in sick. Jacob could use the time alone to work and think.

And pray.

God, this is crazy. Are these thoughts from

You? Am I supposed to be feeling this way about Marissa? It figured the one woman who finally managed to win him over was the one woman who needed to remain off-limits. The image of the chief, dripping wet while Jacob held the telltale water hose in his hand, danced in his vision and he squeezed his eyes shut. Way off-limits. Jacob had real feelings for Marissa, unlike the jerk that Chief had shipped off to Baton Rouge, but in the chief's mind, they were all the same. And now knowing how strained Marissa's relationship was with her father, the chief's overprotective streak made sense. It was a matter of control. And with Marissa, the chief clearly had very little.

He started the truck and welcomed the blast of air-conditioning that cooled his neck. He leaned against the seat with a sigh, gripping the steering wheel with both hands and staring unseeing at the driveway in front of him. It'd been two days since dinner at his brother's house, and Jacob kicked himself every night for not telling Marissa what had been on the tip of his tongue before he started playing with the kids. *I wish*...was all he'd gotten out, and probably that was already too much. What did he wish? He wished he could sweep Marissa off her feet, treat her the way the princess inside her deserved to be treated. Wished he could pursue her without fear of offending the chief and losing his job, and therefore letting down his brother. Wished he could have Marissa's blessing to not only get to know her better, but Owen, too.

Wished she was over her late husband and ready to pursue love again.

Jacob shifted the truck into Drive. His wishes were irrelevant, because reality was reality. As much as Marissa deserved to be a princess, he wasn't cut out to be her shining knight. If it was meant to be, the path would be easier.

Says who? his conscience fairly barked at him as Jacob flipped on his blinker to turn left at the stop sign. What if that wasn't true? What if some things were worth fighting for?

What if the path was somehow cleared?

Jacob accelerated around the curve, unable to dodge the fact that Your Special Day—and Marissa—sat only about six blocks to his right. A new series of what-ifs played out in his mind. What if he told Marissa exactly what he thought and felt? What if she could somehow talk to her father and get his blessing on their relationship so it wasn't an issue?

Without further thought, Jacob yanked the wheel to the right, barely remembering the trailer attached to the truck, and gunned it toward Your Special Day. One thing was certain, even if this entire spontaneous plan blew up in his face. He couldn't spend another night—or meal, for that matter—imagining what could have been.

The truck bounced over the curb into the parking lot of Your Special Day and he double-parked before hurrying out of the cab. He shut the door, then glanced down at the old fire department T-shirt he wore and almost climbed back inside. But he had to do this. Marissa would feel the way she felt about his wardrobe, and this was the time to find out.

Jacob strode purposefully up the walkway, his stomach gnawing with anticipation. Good thing he hadn't had lunch yet. He neared the door and his mouth went dry. *Come on, man. This is Marissa. You can do this.* But he couldn't get the imagery out of his mind of Marissa as a princess, waiting in her castle for a prince. He shook his head in disgust. He'd definitely spent too much time listening to Olivia talk about her party, if these were the thoughts that clamored for his attention.

But he couldn't forget the look in Marissa's eyes at the party supply store when he'd made that princess for a day comment. The truth of her desire to be just that lurked beneath the paper-thin guard of her neutral expression.

Jacob straightened his shoulders and placed his hand on the doorknob, determined to slay any dragons Marissa needed—regardless of the cost.

* * *

"Festival food supplies, check," Marissa muttered from her spot on the floor in her office, nestled between a giant box of red, white and blue paper plates, cups and napkins, and a slightly smaller box of yet-to-be-inflated pink and silver balloons. She made a notation on her legal pad. "Olivia's party balloons, check."

She'd given up on not talking to herself hours ago, when Liz had to leave at noon to take Olivia to an appointment. On her way out, Liz had casually mentioned Ryan was at a job interview, but Marissa could tell from the light in her eyes she hoped it would bring good news. Marissa couldn't imagine losing her entire career and living off savings. It had to be terrifying, especially with a child to support. She knew that feeling. Hopefully this festival would help not only the Greenes, but the other families affected as well.

The shop door opened and Marissa jumped, clutching her legal pad to her chest. Jacob strolled inside, and she did a double take at his rumpled appearance as she tried to stand. Her ankle rolled and she grappled for the side of the nearest box to catch herself, just as Jacob cleared the space between them and steadied her with a firm hand on her arm.

"Sorry. I didn't mean to make such a dramatic

entrance." Jacob smiled down at her, the scent of sweat, grass and spicy aftershave filling her senses. Marissa drew a shaky breath at their proximity. His hand remained on her arm even now that she stood steadily on both feet, and the contact sent sparks all the way up to her shoulder.

She looked away from his dimples and tried to smile back. "No harm done. I got up too fast. Been sitting here awhile."

Jacob took a step back, his fingers skimming the length of her arm before releasing her. She shivered, then tucked her hair behind her ears in an effort to hide her reaction.

Jacob glanced around the brightly lit room, the hum of the fluorescent lights nearly deafening in the charged silence. "Where's Liz?"

"Appointment for Olivia. She mentioned Ryan had an interview today." Marissa felt safe enough to look directly at Jacob now that several feet remained between them. She gestured toward the boxes she'd been inventorying. "She was supposed to help me unpack and organize, hence the chaos."

"Looks like you have it under control." Jacob squatted down to view the contents of the boxes, and Marissa slowly sank back to her original sitting position. "Olivia will love those balloons."

"Will you love blowing them up?" Marissa laughed at Jacob's exaggerated grimace. "I'm kidding. I'll get a helium tank so they'll float." She studied him studying the boxes, and her smile faded. He hadn't come here to talk about balloons. Marissa licked her lips, and hesitated before asking the question burning the back of her throat. "So, did you need something?"

Jacob looked up in surprise, as if he'd just realized he'd been staring aimlessly, and shrugged. "I thought I'd check on the status of the party plans, see if you needed anything else last minute." He rocked forward into a kneeling position, as if he planned on staying a little while.

"I think we're almost ready. But thanks. You've done a lot."

"Actually…" Jacob hesitated. "There is something else."

Marissa raised her eyebrows, and her heart began to pound. She took a deep breath. "Something about Olivia's party? Or the festival?"

"Something about you." His voice lowered and he reached out and tucked a strand of hair behind her ear. "About us."

Marissa's thudding heart relocated to her throat. She opened her mouth but couldn't speak. Could barely breathe.

Jacob's hand trailed from her ear to her chin before his hands landed back in his lap. "Here's the thing. I can't get you out of my head. And trust me, I've tried."

She shook her head, panic rising in her stomach. "Jacob, don't—"

"It's too late." Jacob stood and pulled her up beside him before she could protest. He placed a gentle finger against her lips. "Don't tell me you don't feel this, too. Want this, too."

Marissa lowered her head and closed her eyes, relishing his warmth and nearness. She wanted nothing more than to wrap her arms around his broad shoulders and return the embrace he'd cautiously began. But a relationship between them was a dead-end road. Surely he saw that.

"Don't you feel it?" His voice dropped to a husky whisper and his breath tickled her hair. For a moment, she forgot the myriad reasons why it wouldn't work between them and didn't resist as he tugged her closer, one hand on her waist, the other now sliding behind her neck into her hair. Her heart jump-started in her chest. He was going to kiss her. When was her last kiss? She couldn't even remember. It'd been a long time. Much too long.

Jacob drew nearer, his lips now inches from hers. Her fingers curled into the fabric of his T-shirt, almost as if they had a will of their own. She opened her eyes—and stared directly at the logo on his shirt.

The Orchid Hill Fire Department logo.

Marissa's hands dropped to her sides as if she'd been burned and she took a big step backward. Hurt and confusion etched Jacob's face as he slowly folded his now empty arms across his chest. The motion concealed the logo, but she'd seen it long enough to be reminded of the heartache that would inevitably come if she'd allowed herself to take things further.

"I can't—I'm not…this isn't—" Her flustered thoughts couldn't escape and she gestured helplessly between the two of them. "We just can't—"

"I'm sorry. I'm rushing you." Jacob raked his hands through his hair and began to pace the floor. "I know you're still grieving your husband, and here I am trying to— Man, I'm a jerk. I only wanted you to know how I felt." He stopped and stared at her, his eyes reflecting the same longing she felt to her very core. "I crossed a line."

"No, you didn't." The words fled her lips and she almost clamped a hand over her mouth to stop the denial. He had crossed a line. But not in the way he thought. "I'm not grieving Kevin. Not like you think."

Jacob's head tilted. "But the breakdown you had at church—I thought you missed him."

Her words echoed back at her as loudly as they'd seemed to in the church lobby last Sunday. *I haven't been to church since Kevin died. It was harder than I thought.* No wonder he'd gotten that impression. "You don't understand."

"No, I don't." Jacob took a step toward her, and then stopped as if remembering her rejection anew. "I came here because I thought maybe you could talk to your father. Explain things to him, see if he could stand the idea of us together." Sadness darkened his blue eyes into a melancholy navy. "But you're not ready."

"Jacob." She wanted to explain, but what would it matter? Even if the chief gave his blessing, which was somewhat of a long shot considering their shaky relationship, she couldn't do it. Not as long as that logo remained a part of Jacob's daily wardrobe.

He waited for her to continue, but when she didn't, he nodded slowly. "I'll get out of your way." He turned, his back a rigid line as he slipped outside. The chirping bell on the door proved a stark contrast to the mood that lingered in his absence.

Marissa sank to the floor, her palms still sweaty and her heart still racing from Jacob's honesty. She wanted that kiss. Wanted what he wanted—a relationship. Wanted what they both felt and couldn't deny any longer. But could she risk everything again? How could she trust that anything would be different this time? She hadn't been able to trust Kevin to make wise decisions at work. She couldn't trust her father to value his daughter and family above his job. And she couldn't trust God to keep any of the men in her life safe.

Marissa leaned back against the supply box, clamped both hands over her face and sobbed.

Chapter Twelve

❧

"What do you do when you get rejected by a woman?" Jacob pushed his wet mop across the bay floor toward Steve and watched the shiny trail form against the concrete. "I figure you've had more practice with it." He grinned.

"Very funny." Steve dodged the mop's soaking strings and sidled past the fire truck to the bucket, where he'd been sponging a particularly stubborn grease stain on the floor. Then he smirked back. "Let's ask Captain."

"Right." Jacob snorted. "So, if you ask a woman out and she turns you down, do you take the hint and move on? Or keep pursuing her?"

"Is this a trick question? Some ex-girlfriend of mine hiding in the truck or something?" Steve's eyes narrowed as he cast a cautious glance around the bay, his newly filled sponge dripping on his work pants as he crouched beside the stain.

"No, I'm serious." Jacob stopped mopping and leaned forward, resting part of his weight against the handle. "I'm really asking."

"Man, you must have it pretty bad to ask me for advice." Steve's eyebrows shot up and his scrubbing arm stilled.

"Exactly." Steve had no idea. Jacob had never really had reason to ask anyone's opinion before. He didn't date much, but in the past when he did, he'd always been the one to break it off with the woman, not the other way around. And he couldn't talk to Ryan about it, or Liz would be all over him—Jacob knew better than to think his brother could ever keep a secret from his wife. That was one complication he didn't need, especially after dinner the other night at their house with Liz's not-so-subtle matchmaking attempts.

Attempts that worked—at least on his side.

Steve's head tilted to one side. "Who's the chick?"

Jacob shook his head. "Not important." That was the last thing he could admit to anyone at work.

"Whatever." Steve shrugged. "I guess it depends on the situation. If I barely know her and she says no, I forget it. Everyone strikes out sometimes. But if it's a friend or someone I'm trying to get to know better, then I might keep at it for a while until I'm sure she's not playing hard to get."

That didn't help. Marissa wasn't either scenario—or actually, she was sort of both. He hesitated. "What if it's neither circumstance?"

Steve resumed scrubbing. "Then I'd say bag it and keep shopping."

Jacob frowned. He was a lot of things, but he wasn't a quitter. At this point, he didn't think he could give up on Marissa even if he wanted to. His heart spoke even louder than his smarting pride from her rejection yesterday. The problem was what to do about it. He sighed. "Thanks."

"I didn't help much, huh?"

"Well, I wouldn't recommend starting your own talk show."

Steve laughed. "Hey, live and learn, man. It's the only real advice out there. Do what you feel is best. If I said something you didn't want to hear, then maybe that's not the right answer for you."

"Are you telling me to follow my heart?"

"If I said something that mushy, I'd definitely have my own show." Steve tossed his sponge back in the bucket and wiped his hands on his pants. "But it's good advice, regardless."

Jacob nodded slowly. "Maybe so." The problem was determining exactly what his heart was saying and what God was saying—and if there was a difference. Then again, it might not matter. If Marissa had wanted to become something more, had wanted to kiss him, had wanted to open that door into a real relationship, then

she wouldn't have turned him down yesterday.
But she had looked just as disappointed as he felt
when he left. Something was holding her back
from him. Was it Owen? Was she still upset about
Jacob's unintentional role in her son's life? Maybe
he should back off and give her space—obviously
the flowers had served as more of a complication
than an apology.

But what if she was playing hard to get, as
Steve suggested? As soon as the thought entered
his mind, Jacob shoved it back out. There was no
way. Marissa wasn't into games—she was a working, single mother. Her entire life was responsibility and obligation.

Which made her deserve to be pursued that
much more.

His coworker's voice broke into Jacob's inter-
nal dilemma as Steve headed for the station door.
"Whoever she is, hope it works out." He winked
as he pulled on the knob. "And I hope she can
cook."

Marissa stuck the final candle in Olivia's shim-
mery pink birthday cake as high-pitched, de-
lighted shrieks erupted from the living room,
where a dozen first graders battled it out with a
princess piñata. Her head pounded slightly at the
temples, but so far, the party was a success. Liz
didn't look stressed in the least, and that fact alone

was what kept Marissa moving quietly behind the scenes, taking pictures, picking up trash, announcing games that Liz supervised and refilling punch cups.

Jacob had slipped in a few minutes after the guests arrived, given Olivia a hug and deposited a ridiculously large gift on the hearth before disappearing into the kitchen, where Ryan and the rest of Olivia's extended family congregated, safe from the chaos of seven-year-old, sugar-filled partiers. Thankfully he hadn't sought Marissa out—but was he avoiding her? She wasn't sure which would be worse.

The telltale splatter of candy dropping to Liz's hardwood floor and resounding cheers announced the game was over. Marissa quickly ignited the lighter in her hand and held it over one of the seven purple, glittery candles. The cake was next on the agenda, followed by gifts. Then goody bags would be passed out and hopefully the parents would be on time picking up their kids so Marissa could gain a head start helping Liz clean up.

"That looks nice." Jacob's warm voice behind Marissa burned more intensely than the flames on the cake. She looked up as he rounded the kitchen table to stand beside her, more attractive than ever in jeans and a baby-blue polo shirt that made his eyes nearly electric.

"Thanks." She kept her voice level and her attention on the next candle, despite the spark igniting in her stomach. "But it's not like I made it." Their first conversation since the near-kiss at Your Special Day, and they were going to discuss cake decorations? She tightened her suddenly sweaty grip on the lighter and moved to the next candle. Not that a confrontation would be any easier on her shot nerves.

"Well, hey, you ordered it." Jacob leaned casually against the back of one of the dining room chairs and draped one arm across the top.

"That's like telling someone she's a good cook for sliding a frozen pan of lasagna in the oven." She laughed, but it sounded forced and strange to her own ears. Could he tell she was thinking about their almost kiss? She eased a few steps closer to reach the last candle, her hand trembling. *Stop it. Stop it!*

"Then chalk it up to good taste." He straightened, his eyes lingering on hers before dropping to her lips and back up.

Her stomach flip-flopped and she opened her mouth twice before anything could come out. "Time for cake!" she hollered toward the living room, her gaze never leaving Jacob's. Understanding and something akin to determination flickered in his eyes, and he slowly eased away from the table.

Jacob's light touch on the small of her back as

he passed behind her on his way into the kitchen almost made Marissa drop the lighter. She drew a shuddering breath and pasted on a smile as the swinging doors opened and Olivia and her friends barreled through.

The next fifteen minutes were filled with singing, cake specifications ("I want a corner piece," "No icing please," "Her piece is bigger than mine!") and generous scoops of ice cream. Marissa finally snagged a piece of cake for herself and leaned against the far wall of the living room as Olivia tore into her pile of presents on the fireplace hearth.

Jacob came to stand beside her, a mug of coffee in his hands she'd brewed earlier for the adults. "You've done a really great job. And don't tell me you only ordered everything."

Marissa smiled around her forkful of cake. "Busted. I'll just say thank you."

"I'm serious." Jacob shifted his weight so his upper body angled toward her, his steaming mug clenched between both hands. "I know this was a lot of work, and stressful being last minute, but it's been amazing." He hesitated. "You're pretty amazing."

Marissa's breath hitched and she kept her eyes trained on Olivia as she excitedly pulled a new Barbie doll out of a pile of crinkled wrapping paper. "Just doing my job." She wished she could dive into the compliment and wrap it around herself like a comforting quilt, burrow beneath its warmth and wear it as a reminder that Jacob *saw* her. He'd always seen her, brought out the pieces of her that were generally skipped over due to time restraints or motherly obligation. Instead, she opened her eyes and steeled her shoulders before forking another bite of cake.

"Is this how it's going to be?"

Marissa turned in surprise and met Jacob's saddened expression as he leaned toward her, their faces close. Her heart stuttered and she looked away, then back. "I—I don't know what to say." She knew what she wanted to say. But couldn't. Unfortunately nothing was any different today than it was in her office yesterday. Or the week before that. Tears burned the back of her eyelids but she refused to swipe at them and give herself away. She focused on Liz's happy smile instead as she helped her daughter stack toys on the hearth and reach for another present.

"It's all right. You don't have to say anything at all." Jacob took a sip as he eased away from her to watch Olivia open his gift. A slow smile tilted the corners of his mouth. "But know I'm not giving up."

The tears blurring Marissa's vision dissipated as Jacob's promise melted her defenses, just as quickly as the flames had melted the candles on the birthday cake. Warmth stirred in her middle and rose to her chest. Even after her rejection of his kiss yesterday, even though he assumed she was still grieving her late husband, he wasn't going to stop caring. Stop giving. Stop trying.

And she didn't want him to.

When was the last time anyone had ever deemed her worthy of waiting for? When had anyone cared that much? She'd known Jacob a matter of weeks and yet in one sentence he'd packed more honesty and feeling than years of commitment could hold.

Marissa reached forward and set her cake plate on the end table by the couch. Her empty hands trembled with the memory of being curled into Jacob's shirt against his chest just a day before, tucked in close to his heart. Could she put aside her fears? If he found her worth waiting for, worth pursuing, wasn't he worth risking? Her emotions and logic battled yes and no, and with a dry mouth, she turned to face Jacob, her heart pounding in her throat so loudly she was sure he'd hear it.

She drew a steadying breath, unsure if she'd regret the words she had to say but certain she had to get them out regardless. She rested her hand on his arm, and he looked down at her with a start, a mixture of hope and curiosity in his silvery blue eyes. The chatter of the kids exclaiming over Olivia's gifts faded to the background as they stared at each other. "Jacob, I—"

Three shrill beeps pierced the air, emanating from the pager on Jacob's belt. He shoved his coffee mug in her hands and tugged the pager free from his waist, his face tightening as he read the message scrolling across the screen. "Four-alarm fire downtown. I've got to go."

Marissa's mouth snapped closed as Jacob rushed to plant a kiss on Olivia's head and whispered a quick goodbye to Liz and Ryan. He swiped his keys off the bar stool counter behind Marissa, pain pinching his eyebrows into a jagged line. "We'll talk later?"

Desperation laced his words, and Marissa nodded numbly even though they both knew she wouldn't. The words that had just seconds ago filled her heart to overflowing now lay gasping for breath at the bottom of a dry well, drained of feeling the instant that pager shrieked. The moment had passed.

"Be careful." Marissa bit her tongue, but it was too late. Her warning hovered between them like a dense fog, carrying the same desperation as Jacob's plea to talk later.

"Always." He touched her chin briefly, his gaze heavy and full of something she didn't quite understand, and then he was gone.

Equal measures of pain and relief filled Ma-

rissa's chest as the front door clicked shut behind
Jacob. She stared down into his nearly empty
mug of coffee, the dark liquid barely covering
the bottom of the cup. That'd been close, even
closer than the near-kiss from yesterday. Jacob
had somehow burrowed under her defenses, and
her carefully constructed wall was crumbling. If
she'd told him she wasn't grieving Kevin, if she'd
spoken the words he'd wanted to hear and convinced him she felt ready for a relationship, ready
to move on—with him—she'd feel even worse
than she did now.

Wouldn't she?

Because if she and Jacob pursued whatever it
was between them, this would be her life—again.
Empty dining room chairs where Dad was supposed to sit at dinnertime. Missed recitals and
birthday parties and rushing off from New Year's
celebrations because some idiot across town didn't
use fireworks responsibly. Asking for Da-Da at
bedtime but getting the same tired answer over
and over. She couldn't put herself and Owen
through that another time.

Even if the decision not to hurt almost as badly.

"You okay?" Liz mouthed the words from the
hearth as she helped Olivia open her last present,
her eyes darting from Marissa to the front door
and back again.

Marissa nodded, forcing a smile she didn't feel,

as Jacob's truck started outside. The tires squealed as he floored it down the driveway and to the street, burning rubber toward a fire.

And away from her.

Chapter Thirteen

No woman could turn down a cookie bouquet, could they? Jacob studied the arrangement of glazed, heart-shaped sugar cookies behind the glass counter. The arrangement, once completed, would mirror those displayed on the countertop, each cookie pierced with a wooden stick and nestled in a vase like a bouquet of flowers.

Jacob nodded at the woman behind the counter, who stood at the ready with parchment paper and a plastic-gloved hand. "A dozen, like those in that arrangement." He pointed to the ones he wanted and waited with a knot in his stomach while she prepared the bouquet. This had to be either the best idea he'd ever had or the corniest—probably both. Time would tell, along with Marissa's reaction.

Jacob watched the cookies take shape into a flowery form at the clerk's careful touch. He and Marissa hadn't spoken since the party last Saturday. Even yesterday at church she'd seemed withdrawn, sitting on the end of the pew by Liz and staring straight ahead, sadness pinching the corners of her mouth as she listened to the preacher. She'd slipped out to gather Owen from his class and was halfway to her SUV before he could even clear the congested crowd filtering through the double doors of the foyer.

Maybe Marissa would eventually soften toward him like the glaze on the baked cookies. He knew better than to get his hopes too high, though—the look on her face as he'd headed out the door at Olivia's party had said far more than he'd wanted to hear. He'd reminded her of her aversion to fireman, and in the worst possible way. It burned him up inside that he had to leave his niece's party— the very party he paid for and helped arrange— but duty was duty. Olivia understood—after all, her dad had done the same thing more times than he could count before his layoff. So why couldn't Marissa?

"Fifty-six forty-two." The clerk smiled and held out her hand, now free of the glove, as Jacob tugged his wallet from his pants pocket.

"Ouch." A deep voice behind him chuckled. "Watch out if you put loose change back in that wallet. There's got to be a hole in there now."

Jacob turned to find Chief Brady standing behind him in uniform, a slight grin breaking his typical stern expression. Jacob's stomach dropped as he held out his hand in a handshake, hoping his grip didn't reveal the sudden shakiness taking over his body. "Nice to see you, Chief." Maybe the chief wouldn't ask who the cookies were for. He couldn't lie—but man, he couldn't admit the truth, either. It was one thing for him and Marissa to approach the chief together about a relationship, quite another for Jacob to admit his feelings when he hadn't even won Marissa's heart yet. Talk about getting shot down before even having a chance.

"Sir?" The woman behind the counter waited with raised eyebrows.

Jacob startled, then quickly dropped the bills into the clerk's outstretched palm, the cookies blurring in his vision. *Hurry up, hurry up.* He forced a smile, like this was any other purchase.

"I'll be right with you." The woman smiled at the chief as she counted out Jacob's change.

Chief Brady nodded. "No hurry, Betty. I need two of those lemon bars, as usual." He turned and clapped a hand on Jacob's shoulder so hard Jacob winced. "Don't worry, son. They'll be worth it. Women like sweets."

Apparently so did the chief, judging by the size of the lemon bars Betty was packaging. Jacob scooped his cookie basket off the counter, relief flooding his senses that the chief wasn't prying for names. "See you around, Chief."

He hesitated at the door, wondering if he should apologize again for the water hose incident, when the chief pocketed his change and took the white paper bag from Betty. Jacob mentally kicked himself for the distraction. Now they'd have to walk out together or it'd be rude.

The chief slowly ambled toward the door Jacob held open, taking a bite of lemon bar before he even reached the parking lot. "So who's the lucky lady?"

Panic gripped Jacob's heart in a vice and his hands tightened on the basket in a near death grip. He opened his mouth, then closed it. "Someone I met recently."

"Wow, these lemon bars are to die for." The chief reached for the second one as he neared his car. "You ever had one?"

Jacob practically wilted with relief at the change of subject, much like the sugar cookies were beginning to do in the sun bearing down on his forearms. "No, can't say that I have." He shifted the arrangement to his other arm and pulled his truck keys from his pocket.

"I'm a regular around here." Chief Brady nodded at the package Jacob held. "Hope those work out for you."

"Thank you, sir."

The chief opened his door. "When do you work next?"

"I go back on Wednesday." That left Jacob only today and tomorrow to devote his time to Marissa—and finishing his duties for the upcoming festival, which was now less than a week away. Funny how time flew when doing something you enjoyed—in the presence of someone you enjoyed even more.

"Keep an eye out, you hear? Anything suspicious at the stations, I want to know about it." The chief slid into his car and cranked the ignition before Jacob could question his meaning. Anything suspicious as in an irate citizen starting fires because of the layoffs? Or suspicious as in a fireman falling for the chief's daughter?

Jacob lifted one hand in a wave to the chief before buckling the cookie basket into the passenger seat of his truck. Even before the water hose incident at the station and his feelings for Marissa, Chief Brady had been a force to reckon with. He seemed harmless enough on the outside, but his demeanor and stature were at times downright intimidating. Jacob couldn't help wondering what it would be like to have the chief as a father—certainly not easy.

He swung into the cab and started his truck. Maybe that was why firemen in general left a bad taste in Marissa's mouth. It couldn't have been easy living that life as a kid. The chief was married to his work, a fact Jacob both respected and disdained for various reasons. He could understand the motivation behind that level of commitment—it'd served the chief well for his career. But at what cost?

Perhaps that was the reason for the fearful anger in Marissa's eyes every time she recalled Jacob's interaction with Owen, and Owen's constant chattering about becoming a fireman. Still, that didn't seem like enough reason for the reactions she'd given these past few weeks. Owen wasn't heading off to college and making career choices yet. He was seven.

Yet something sparked in Marissa's eyes every time Jacob's career was mentioned—or, as it'd been at Olivia's party—shoved in her face.

Jacob steered his truck toward Spruce Street and Your Special Day, and shot a glance at the bouquet beside him. "I sure hope you work," he muttered. But something told him it was going to take a lot more than cookies to break the barrier around Marissa's carefully protected heart.

Hopefully his wallet would be able to keep up.

"Can you believe these letters to the editor?" Marissa flicked the pages of the local newspapers to straighten them and furrowed her brow at Liz, who snagged a bottle of water from the fridge by Marissa's desk.

"What is it this time? More 'unfair' complaints about the layoffs?" Liz twisted off the top and gave a wry smile before taking a sip. "I could write a book about unfair, trust me."

So could she. Marissa smiled back. "These are going a step further than the letters we've been seeing. I'm almost surprised they're printing them." She gestured with her chin. "Listen to this one. 'Dear Editor, I must say I'm ashamed to live in a city where not only are honest, hardworking firemen let go for budget cuts, but to watch the very creators of said budget drive around town in sports cars. I'm betting their shoes are new, too.'"

Liz snorted and nearly choked on her water. "That's a good one. What else?"

Marissa turned the page. "'Dear Editor, the city council and mayor might be relieved to ease the stress of budget concerns by laying off local firemen, but how stressed are they going to be when they need backup for an emergency and it isn't there?'"

Liz nodded. "Good point."

"You're so civil about this." Marissa peered over the top page of the paper. "Were you tempted to write some of the same stuff?"

"Not at all." Liz closed her water bottle and settled into the chair across from Marissa. "It is what it is. It's nice to hear the community standing up for us families, but truthfully, I'd rather have them contribute to things like the festival and fundraising than I would them fight fire with fire—pardon the pun—and stir up rumors of fraud."

"I'm afraid this person doesn't agree with you." Marissa continued reading. "'Dear Editor, I don't think the city council and mayor realize what they've gotten themselves into. This entire situation is going to backfire and it's going to happen quickly. You can be certain they'll regret their rash decisions.'"

"That almost sounds threatening." Liz frowned. "Do you think it's connected to the arson fire downtown a few weeks ago?"

"Don't be silly. I doubt an arsonist would be stupid enough to blab to the newspaper and give any hint of what he'd done—if it was even connected to the layoffs in the first place. There's no proof at all one way or the other yet."

Liz shrugged. "Maybe, but maybe not. These letters are anonymous, you know. Even the newspaper wouldn't realize who sent them if they were mailed in with no return address."

"You sound as paranoid as my father." Marissa folded the newspaper and slid it into the top drawer of her desk. "By the way, how did you know about the arson? I thought Dad was going to keep that under wraps."

"Ryan still has friends. You know firemen—they're brothers for life." Liz smiled. "For better or for worse—and trust me, we're in the worst."

Marissa wrinkled her nose in sympathy. "How are you guys doing?"

"Financially?" Liz exhaled. "We're getting by."

"I wish I could afford to pay you for your work here. You've been a lifesaver." Marissa motioned to her nearly clean desk. "I forgot my desk was brown."

"I wouldn't take the money if you handed it to me. You've done more than enough for us, planning this festival and working on Olivia's party last minute. Which, by the way, she's still talking about." Liz grinned. "The pin the tail on the pony was priceless. And I'm still finding wrapped candy in my couch cushions from the piñata burst."

"Yeah, that should have been a backyard game, in hindsight." Marissa laughed.

Outside, a truck rumbled to a stop in the parking lot and Liz stood up to peer out the window. "Sounds like Jacob's truck. Ryan's always jealous of how loud it is compared to his pickup."

Marissa's heart skipped and she pressed a hand to her stomach, wishing it wouldn't be immature to hide in the bathroom or stockroom until he left. Her mouth went dry as a car door slammed and heavy footsteps sounded on the walk. She had to be professional, for the sake of the festival and her own sanity. So what if she had almost confessed her heart's desires to him last weekend? She hadn't, and he'd made her choice even easier by reminding her of all the reasons they didn't belong together—beginning and ending with that pager clipped to his belt and the logo on his shirt she could still feel under her fingertips.

The door opened and Jacob strolled inside, a towering bouquet of cookies in his hand. "Afternoon, ladies."

"What in the world?" Liz stood to peer at the arrangement Jacob set on the desk in front of Marissa.

"I figured you deserved some flowers that wouldn't die." He smiled at Marissa, and her stomach flickered in response. "Of course, they wouldn't stick around long enough to wilt even if they could. My truck smells like a rolling bakery now. I'm assuming they taste as good as they smell."

Marissa gently touched one of the wrapped cookies on a stick. "They're—perfect." Like Jacob. Thoughtful. Unique. Sweet.

"And sticky." Liz plucked a cookie from the vase, unwrapped the plastic and took a bite. "Oh, wow. These are great."

Marissa's fingers hovered over the arrangement, wanting to try one but unable to shake the thought that eating one would demonstrate an acceptance she wasn't ready to give. Would it send the wrong message? Her stomach growled, and she remembered she'd skipped lunch. *Come on, Marissa. It's only a cookie. Not a promise ring.* She took a heart-shaped cookie from a stick and took a slow bite, unable to look away from Jacob's smile as he settled into the empty chair beside Liz.

"So what's on the agenda for today festival wise?" Jacob checked his watch. "You ladies have me for about two hours before I have to run some errands for my lawn service."

Grateful he wasn't pressing the issue of the gift, Marissa finished her cookie and wiped her hands on her jeans before thumbing open her planner. "Everything is coming together pretty well. But I'm still waiting to hear from the funnel cake vendor. Liz, you want to give them a call? The festival is Saturday, they can't put off their decision any longer and I'd really like those cakes to be there. They'd be a big seller."

"I'm on it." Liz popped the last bite of her cookie in her mouth and mumbled around the crumbs. "Hand me the phone. They'll be there."

Marissa traded places with Liz so she could make the call and sat beside Jacob, hoping he didn't notice the chemistry she felt sizzling between them like two pieces of bacon in a frying pan. "As for you..." Her voice trailed off as she skimmed her list. "Would you rather confirm details with the chalk box artist or check with the live band to make sure they're still coming?"

"I'll call the band." Jacob glanced at Liz, whose back was turned in the desk chair as she sweet-talked the funnel cake vendor into coming at a discount. "But first..." He took Marissa's hand and gave it a soft squeeze. "I just wanted to give you the chance to finish what you were going to say at Olivia's party. Before we were interrupted."

Marissa looked at their joined hands, wanting simultaneously to tug away and twine her fingers through his. How could she feel a pull so strongly in two completely different directions? She had to remain strong, and not let her emotions take over what she knew would only end in heartache. "Jacob, I can't."

"Can't what?" He didn't let go, but absently rubbed his thumb over her palm.

A shiver started at the base of her neck and traveled down her spine, and she gently pulled her hand free. "I can't talk about this right now. I have work to do."

Jacob appraised her with a lingering glance before reaching forward and taking a cookie from the bouquet. "And apparently, so do I."

* * *

"Owen, did you clean up your room?" Marissa shut the dishwasher with a snap and cranked the dial to Start.

"Yes, Mom," Owen called from the living room. "Twice!"

"Well, that's because you messed it up again right after." Marissa smiled as she wiped the counters by the sink. She tossed the wet paper towel into the trash can, then rounded the corner into the living room. Her smile faded at the toy fire truck Owen raced around the living room floor. "Hey, why don't we play a board game? Or work a puzzle?" She worked to keep the tension from her voice. Why couldn't Owen play with the race cars she'd bought him? Or the train set her mom had got him last month?

"Puzzles are for girls."

"Since when?" Marissa frowned.

He looked up long enough to smirk. "Since Olivia said she got three for her birthday."

Marissa opened her mouth to argue, then closed it. Some battles weren't worth fighting. "Then what about a game? Chutes and Ladders? Go Fish?"

"Nah, you'll just let me win. I like my fire truck." He made a high-pitched siren noise as he scooted the truck under the coffee table, beside the end table and in circles around Marissa's feet.

She looked down, literally surrounded by her worst nightmare, and closed her eyes. The urge to pray welled in her throat but she shoved it back down. God wasn't interested in bailing her out. If He was, He'd have started long before now—like maybe on the night the chief strode up her walkway, hat in his hands, with news she'd already felt in her heart hours before. She'd be foolish to think anything had changed because of her attendance in church the past few weeks.

The phone rang, pulling Marissa from the temptation to throw Owen's fire truck in the backyard. She snatched the phone from its stand, holding one finger over her lips in a failed effort to silence Owen's siren noises. "Hello?" She clamped one hand over her free ear and moved toward her bedroom, away from the chaos of her son and the competing dishwasher.

"Will you believe me now?"

The gruff voice and lack of polite hello could only be her father. Marissa pinched the bridge of her nose. Another lecture—surprise, surprise. "What now, Dad?"

"Someone threw a firebomb into Station 4 a few hours ago."

"What?" Marissa gasped, her hand falling helplessly to her side. She sagged against the wall, heart racing. "Was anyone hurt?" Her mind raced. Jacob. No, wait. He didn't work until Wednesday. And he typically had duty at Station 6. Or was it 7? Her panic slowed along with her heartbeat and she took a calming breath.

Her father cleared his throat. "No, thank goodness. They broke the window to the sleeping quarters, but the guys were on a run."

Marissa closed her eyes in relief. That had to be a shock—coming back from working a fire to see your own station in flames. But at least everyone was okay.

"Two arson situations in less than two weeks. You can't tell me this isn't connected to the layoffs and the letters in the newspaper." The chief's tone darkened. "I saw what people are writing in. They're escalating. Just like the crimes."

"Dad, you're the fire chief. Not the chief of police. Aren't the cops supposed to figure this stuff out?"

"This blurs the lines. Of course they're involved but so is Jackson."

Anthony Jackson was the arson investigator for Orchid Hill, a job that was sort of a joke since they rarely had need for him. He spent more time subbing for vacationing or retiring captains and assistant chiefs than he did detective work—a fact that reminded Marissa how ridiculous her father's theory was in the first place. "Dad, this is Orchid Hill. Not Chicago. We aren't exactly known for our high crime rate."

"Well, Chicago isn't known for laying off their men."

Marissa shoved her free hand into her hair in frustration. "The festival is in a week. I'm not canceling it now, even if it were my call to make. But it's not. The church hired me, and I can assure you they aren't concerned about any of this."

"Because they don't know. I told you, the media reports what we tell them. Or what leaks out."

"Then you better leak something out if you want them to know, because we're running full speed ahead as scheduled."

She almost picture her father's red face as his voice rose. "If we spread the word about what's happening, we'd likely get even more hits because of giving this jerk the attention he wants."

Marissa remembered Liz's comment earlier about Ryan still having connections to information at work, and sighed. "It's already leaking, Dad. Don't worry about the festival." *Or me.* She wished that was his only motivation—but she wasn't naive enough to think her dad would suddenly care after all these years. More likely he was concerned about his own reputation.

"You're a stubborn woman."

She bit her tongue to hold back the retort she

desperately longed to fire. "Good night, Dad." She stabbed the off button with her finger and threw the phone on her bed. It clanked against the headboard with a satisfying thump. Why couldn't she have normal parents? A father who cared, who helped sustain her after tragedy, instead of pushing her further away? A father who wanted to be involved in her life for the right reasons, instead of trying to control or manipulate for his own political advantage?

God, am I destined to lose everyone I've ever cared for?

The prayer slipped unbidden from Marissa's heart. She pictured Owen racing his fire truck around the floor just a few rooms away, and stifled a cry.

Please, no.

She pressed shaking fingers against the tears forming in her eyes and steeled her shoulders. She refused to lose her son—physically, the way she'd lost her husband, or emotionally, the way she'd lost her father. It was up to her to prevent the pattern, to break that cycle of destruction in her family, regardless of the cost. Starting with a toy fire truck.

And ending with her feelings for Jacob.

Chapter Fourteen

❧

"It's been great to see you these past few weeks at service," Pastor Rob said over the phone.

Marissa traded ears with her cell as she flipped on her blinker, guilt pinching her stomach. What would he think if he knew the only reason she went was because of Liz's persistence and Owen's excitement? Could the pastor tell Marissa spent half of the service locked in her own thoughts instead of hearing the sermon? She swallowed. "It's been very…interesting." She wanted to say she enjoyed the services, but that would be stretching the truth. Maybe one day she'd be able to say so sincerely.

If she kept coming.

She forced a smile. "My son really loves his Sunday school class." There, that was honest.

"Glad to hear it. And I'm also glad to hear the festival is coming together under budget." Pastor

Rob chuckled. "If you can keep it that way, our budget committee will be thrilled."

"I'll do my best." Marissa adjusted the rush of air filtering through the car vents to blow on her flushed face. Between the setting sun warming her shoulders through the window and the guilt rushing to her face, she could use some relief. "Thanks for checking in. I'm heading to the volunteers' meeting now."

"Sounds good. We'll talk soon." They hung up, and Marissa dropped her cell in her lap as she turned onto Jacob's country road. Two minivans and several cars already lined his long gravel drive, and she'd never felt more appreciative of company than tonight. Jacob had volunteered to have the meeting at his house so everyone could get a visual of where their booths would be and what they'd need for the big event. Tonight they would also go by and mark off where each booth would be set to make sure everyone had plenty of space. Hopefully they'd stay so busy, she wouldn't think of Jacob in any way other than the nice guy allowing use of his property for a good cause. Not as the man who'd sneaked into her heart when she wasn't looking. Not as the man who'd almost kissed her in her office.

And certainly not as the man she still wanted to kiss despite every fiber of her being knowing better.

Marissa's cheeks flushed hotter and she quickly

parked beside a blue sedan and climbed out of her car, pausing to grab her organizer and tote bag of supplies from the backseat. At least Liz had volunteered to watch Owen at her house with Olivia that night so Marissa could focus on leading the meeting and not worry about Owen running his fire truck all around Jacob's house. That was the last thing she needed—the two of them bonding even further. She'd bit her tongue on more than one occasion since her father's phone call last night. Once when Owen asked when he could see Mr. Jacob again, twice when he repeated a knock-knock joke Jacob had told him at church and thirdly when he commented on how Mr. Jacob could teach him all about real fire trucks.

She climbed the porch steps, noting the fireman's flag on the walkway again, and shook her head in disgust at her own naïveté. If she would have just realized who Jacob was and what he did for a living before she'd fallen for— No, she wouldn't go there. If she admitted the depth of her feelings, there'd be no going back.

And she had to keep moving forward.

Marissa drew a deep breath at the front door before knocking and slowly pushed her way inside. The aroma of freshly baked chocolate chip cookies permeated the house. From the kitchen, sounds of laughter and clinking of ice being poured into glasses filled her ears. She started in that direction, and then hesitated as the photos on the fireplace hearth caught her attention. Jacob, in full uniform at his academy graduation, smiled at her from the mantel, encased in a silver frame. Beside that sat a picture of him and Ryan, again in uniform with a fire truck behind them, cheesing it up for the camera, their arms draped around each other.

She looked away, only to notice the afghan draped across the back of the leather couch—the nationwide firefighter's emblem emblazoned in the fabric. A miniature stone statue of a fireman holding an American flag adorned the end table beside the recliner. A lump knotted in Marissa's throat. Jacob was a fireman, through and through—exactly the way it should be. As much as she'd like things to be different, they simply weren't. The sooner she quit forgetting that, the better.

For both her and Owen.

She quickly made her way to the kitchen, which was open to the living room by means of a bar counter and several stools, now filled with volunteers from the church, who filled glasses and set cookies on a platter. Jacob stood in the middle of the kitchen, his head tilted back in laughter at something the woman in front of him had obviously just said.

Marissa paused, still unnoticed, unable to look

away from the dimples on Jacob's cheeks, his slightly rumpled hair as if he'd raked his fingers through it, the way his forest green polo shirt showcased his biceps.

She adjusted her grip on the tote bag, sudden melancholy rising in her chest. She was an outsider here. She might be the group leader tonight, but she wasn't a part of their church world. Had anyone in this group of congregation members been through the tragedy she'd been through? Had they faced the storms of life and come out the other side clean and dry? Or like her, were they still floundering in the rain, unsure where to go, trying to hide how lost they felt?

They didn't look lost—especially not the pretty brunette giggling at Jacob's side, one manicured hand resting lightly on his forearm.

"Marissa!" Jacob finally saw her, and a rush of warmth filled her stomach as he left the group and rushed to her side. "You're here." He looped an arm around her shoulders and introduced her to the group, his touch burning her upper arm. "Marissa will be in charge tonight, guys. We've got to listen up so we can pull this festival off, all right?"

Marissa pushed away the cozy feeling that came from being tucked against Jacob's side, and eased away. Nice as it was, and as badly as it stung watching him interact with attractive women, he was probably better off with one of them. Someone who considered him the hero he was, someone who could support the profession Marissa promised she'd never again embrace.

"Thanks for coming. If everyone will move into the living room, we'll get started." She clutched her organizer to her chest and tried to smile with sincerity. "We have a lot to cover tonight." She appraised her volunteers, determined to think of them as the kind people they were—volunteering for the cause she'd been hired to direct—and not as a group to which she couldn't belong, and definitely not as competition for Jacob's heart.

That was one battle she wasn't prepared to fight.

Jacob set the last of the dirty coffee mugs in the sink. "You didn't have to stay and help clean up, you know." He took the plate riddled with cookie crumbs from Marissa's outstretched hands and sunk it beneath the soapy water. "You've done enough tonight already." Including making it hard for him to breathe with every toss of her silky hair, but that was almost as corny as Steve's line about following his heart.

Corny—but still incredibly true.

Marissa made her way around the edge of the bar to join him. "I don't mind. I feel strange leaving behind a mess." She smiled. "Must be a mom thing."

He met her smile with one of his own. At least she'd finally loosened up from the stiff, guarded woman who'd edged her way into his house a few hours before. As Marissa stood in front of his fireplace and delegated tasks to volunteers, patiently answered questions and nibbled on chocolate chip cookies, she'd found her element and shone.

He just wished that beaming smile had been directed toward him a few more times.

"I think things are really coming together, don't you? Everyone was very responsive." Marissa handed him a towel, and his fingers brushed hers as he took it and dried his hands.

The contact sent a spark shooting up his arm and he swallowed before tossing the rag back on the counter. "It'd be hard not to be responsive to you."

Marissa's luminous gaze darted to his and then nervously away, and Jacob sighed. "Don't, okay?"

"Don't what?" She kept her gaze on the soap bubbles dissipating in the sink.

He lightly gripped her elbow, letting his fingers slide down the length of her forearm before squeezing her hand. "Don't push me away because I gave you a compliment."

She looked up, and a soft smile turned the corners of her lips. "You saw that one coming a mile away."

"You're getting predictable." He let go of her

hand before it made her uncomfortable, and moved to the fridge. "Soda?"

"Do you have water instead?"

He tossed her a bottle and she caught it with better reflexes than he expected. "Pull up a chair. You've been standing all night." He gestured to the table in the corner of the kitchen and they settled into the chairs.

"There is something I've wanted to ask you." Marissa hesitated, and Jacob's pulse kicked up a notch. Maybe she was finally ready to acknowledge his gifts and the meaning behind them. He took a long swig of soda, determined not to rush her. *Steady, steady. Let her speak.*

"Who do you think is behind the arson fires?"

Jacob jerked in his chair, nearly dropping his soda can. So much for true confessions of the heart. He set his drink on the table and turned to Marissa with raised eyebrows. "Why are you worried about that?"

She shrugged, but concern lurked beneath her expression. "I've heard some—rumors—that make me suspicious."

Rumors…from her dad? He wouldn't ask. But judging by her averted gaze, he'd guess that was the source—meaning they weren't rumors at all, but Chief Brady's real suspicions. He cleared his throat. "I wouldn't be upset about it. I'm sure they'll taper off. The police will catch the guy eventually."

"So you don't think the arson fires are related to the department layoffs?" Marissa played with the cap on her water bottle and finally looked into his eyes.

Now it was his turn to shrug. "I have no idea. I guess anything is possible."

"Do you think the fundraiser is drawing extra attention to the layoffs? Maybe upsetting the wrong person?"

Ah. There was the source of it. She felt guilty. Jacob leaned forward across the table, trying to draw her in. "You're doing a good deed, Marissa. I know how much you cut off your profit to help the church pay for this festival. Don't stress over things you can't control."

"You're right. The—rumors—are just getting to me." She took a deep breath as if fortifying herself for the next question. "Do you think it's possible it could be one of the men who were let go?"

Jacob finished his drink and pitched the can into the wastebasket at the end of the bar. "Trust me, I know those guys personally. There's no way they'd stoop to that level."

"I wouldn't have thought so." She nodded, but didn't seem entirely convinced.

"Firemen are brothers, Marissa. Seriously, it's not possible. Even if one of them would want revenge on the council or the mayor—which I still can't fathom—they wouldn't do it this way. Not to their own men."

"I wish everyone were as confident about that as you." She drank the last of her water, then checked her watch and quickly stood. "I've got to pick up Owen from your brother's house. It's later than I thought."

Jacob stood with her, his chair scraping against the tile floor. "Tell Owen I said hello." He winced at the automatic words. *Great going. Way to remind her of the past when you've finally made some headway.*

Marissa's head tilted to the side, and she gave him what he was coming to think of as her famous appraising stare. "I will," she finally said with a resigned smile. "He'd like that."

Shock radiated up Jacob's backbone, but he kept what he hoped was a nonchalant expression as he walked Marissa to the door. His heart hammered in his chest with every step. Dare he push it further? Or be grateful for the progress they'd made and leave it at that? "Thanks again for helping me clean up."

She shouldered her purse she'd left at the entryway and picked up her planner and empty tote bag. "I enjoyed it."

So did he. It felt right having her in his kitchen, helping him as if they'd hosted the party together.

He wanted more nights like this one. A lot more. Jacob hesitated, then reached out and tucked a loose strand of hair behind her ear. "And thanks for everything else, too."

She held his gaze, nibbling on her lower lip, and nodded slowly as his meaning sunk in. "You're very welcome."

Her voice was barely louder than a whisper, and he wished he had the right to lean in and kiss her. Their near-kiss from that fateful afternoon at Your Special Day had radiated warmth in his stomach that quickly spread into his chest. But he wouldn't push her again. He leaned around her to open the front door. "Let me know if you need help with anything else."

"With?" She eased out onto the porch and turned with raised eyebrows.

Jacob braced his shoulder against the frame, debating how much to reveal. How could he tell her he wanted to be her go-to guy? That he'd be more than willing to come inspect the yard for strange noises in the middle of the night, kill an intimidating bug or unclog a toilet? Maybe not the most romantic of notions, but his feelings for Marissa were diving much deeper than surface level romance. He wanted to be a part of her and Owen's lives—the good and the bad.

For better and for worse.

But that much honesty would send Marissa skittering right off the porch and never coming back. He couldn't risk the progress they'd made. Jacob cleared his throat and smiled, hoping it looked convincing. "With the festival."

Marissa clutched the strap of her tote bag on her shoulder, her knuckles white. "Right. The festival. I'll do that." A disconcerting mixture of relief and disappointment lingered in Marissa's smile. She lifted her hand in a wave. "Good night."

Jacob said good-night, then shut the front door and leaned his forehead against it with a groan.

He knew exactly how she felt.

Chapter Fifteen

"I come bearing gifts." Liz breezed through the door of the fire station and set a platter of brownies on the coffee table, pausing to dump her purse on the end of the couch.

Jacob shut the door behind her. "Thanks, Liz. What did we do to deserve this?" She didn't owe the fire department anything, that was for sure. Jacob pushed away the familiar negativity that would only turn his good day black. He wanted to bask in the positive memories of Marissa at his house last night, not dwell on the things he couldn't change.

Although, really, at this point they were all one and the same.

Steve sat upright from his sprawled position on the couch and plucked a piece of baked chocolate from the tray. "Did Jacob ever tell you the last woman who brought him brownies at work—"

Jacob silenced Steve with a swift kick to his shin.

"Ow." Brownie crumbs sprayed as Steve rubbed the offending spot on his leg. He winked at Liz. "You make one measly joke around here and—"

"We'll be outside," Jacob interrupted. "Try to save me at least one brownie." He steered Liz outside to the bay, where the freshly washed trucks were parked, unwilling for Liz to hear the dish on his former dates and even more unwilling for Steve to hear whatever it was Liz came to say. Because as sweet as his sister-in-law was, she had a motive that had nothing to do with the full bellies of her local fire crew.

"Spill it." Jacob crossed his arms over his chest and waited.

"Spill what? I had the urge to bake last night, that's all. I'm on my way to work at Your Special Day and thought I'd drop some treats here first." Liz gestured to her car parked in the driveway outside the open bay door. "I have a pan in the backseat for Marissa to take home to Owen."

"So you just happened to come here, on your way to see Marissa, and have no ulterior motives?" Jacob steadied his gaze on Liz, and sure enough, she started shifting under the scrutiny.

She huffed. "Fine, have it your way. You know I can't lie."

"And my brother is extra appreciative of that." Jacob chuckled. "So what gives?"

"I'm worried about you both." All traces of humor fled from Liz's eyes, replaced with a heavy veil of concern. "Marissa is good for you, and you're good for her. I know I said I'd back off the matchmaking but this is more serious than that. You guys need each other."

"And you think the fact that we're not together is my fault?" Jacob jabbed his chest, frustration jetting up his spine. "Why don't you give this speech to Marissa?"

"I plan to." Liz crossed her arms and stared up at Jacob. "After I'm done with you."

"I'm trying, Liz. What more do you want from me? What more does Marissa want from me?" Jacob threw his arms out to the sides. "Because obviously my flowers, compliments and cookie bouquets aren't enough. I thought last night after the festival volunteer meeting that we'd had a moment, a connection. But apparently—"

"You did." Liz's quiet confirmation jolted Jacob into silence. "When she came to pick up Owen, it was all over her face. But she was upset. I think she's fighting her feelings for you."

"Then why are you picking on me? I'm not hiding mine."

"Because you need to try harder."

"Well, I'm afraid my wallet can't stand many more attempts at 'courtship,' as you called it." Jacob snorted. A brisk wind blew through the open bay door and cooled his rising temper. He rubbed his temples with both fingers and exhaled a stress-laden breath. "What would you suggest if you were in my shoes? I'm running out of options. I can't push her too far."

The breeze ruffled the ends of Liz's curly hair, pulled back out of her face with a clip. "I don't think you have all the pieces of the puzzle."

"Then enlighten me, please." Jacob leaned back against the fender of one of the trucks.

Liz hesitated, her fingers nervously twirling the wedding ring on her left hand. The rotating diamond flashed in the sun streaming through the doors, and Jacob was once again reminded of his responsibilities to his family. After Ryan was let go, Liz had offered to pawn her ring for grocery money. If not for Jacob stepping in, she might have done it despite Ryan's protests. Some of Jacob's frustration melted away as he studied Liz. She meant well—she always did. She just had control freak tendencies that were often displayed in the most inconvenient ways—like toward his love life. But at this point, he was so desperate he'd do anything to win Marissa's heart and affection—even involving the infamous matchmaker.

"If she hasn't given you the pieces, I'm not sure it's my place to do so."

Jacob let out an exaggerated gasp. "You? Keep a secret?"

"It's not a secret," Liz protested. "Just not my information to share."

"You can't tell me I'm missing something and not tell me what." Jacob shoved his hands in his pants pockets. "Come on, Liz. This is important."

The toe of her boot tapped incessantly against the concrete floor and he waited. *Tap, tap, tap.* She opened her mouth, then closed it. *Tap, tap, tap.* Her wedding ring twirled faster, until Jacob's curiosity built to the bursting point. "Liz!"

"Marissa's late husband was a fireman. He died in the line of duty." The words blurted from her lips but that was all Jacob heard as the rest of the station sounds evaporated into a deafening silence. Blood pulsed in his ears, giving him the sensation of being underwater. Fireman…fireman… fireman… The word echoed in his brain, until he closed his eyes in a useless effort to drown it out. He'd just thought Marissa's dad was his obstacle. Now he was up against a late husband and an entire marriage of memories.

Any hope he had of convincing Marissa to give him a chance disappeared into the afternoon shadows now filling the bay.

"Thanks again for the brownies." Marisa took a big bite and wiped her hands on her pants, glad she'd worn work jeans to the office today. She checked her fingers for chocolate stains before flipping through the pages of the planner opened on her lap. "They were just the pick-me-up I needed after scheduling those two anniversary parties."

Liz perched on the edge of Marissa's desk and tapped the planner with her finger. "How will you manage pulling those off with the festival, too?"

"These clients were very clear on what they wanted, so it's not a lot of creative work. I can still focus on the festival, and after Saturday, I can move my attention to the new parties." Marissa finished her brownie and shrugged. "I can't turn away the money right now. I've already lost a little on this because of the discount—" She stopped abruptly and heat flooded her neck.

"I know you're sacrificing your time you could be spending on other events to do the festival." Liz offered a grateful smile. "I can't tell you how much that means to us."

Marissa brushed off Liz's gratitude with a wave of her hand. "Don't think twice about it. Here, you can help me file if it makes you feel better." She grinned and handed Liz half the stack of invoices that needed to be stored in the filing cabinet.

Liz took the pile and began to sort it. "Olivia can't stop talking about the festival. She's really looking forward to the chalk boxes the artist is drawing up."

"I'm hoping those will be a big hit," Marissa

agreed. "Although Owen will probably be determined to draw a fire truck in his." She sighed, not
willing to delve into that unsavory topic yet again.
Owen kept talking about Jacob at home—and in
the car, and at church, and pretty much at every
other waking moment. Which was only fair since
Jacob was invading her thoughts almost as often.
She forced a smile—and a change of subject. "So
how did Ryan's interview go last week?"

"He hasn't heard yet, but he's hopeful." Liz
thumbed through the stack in her lap. "It was a
little weird being at the station, to be honest."

Marissa raised her eyebrows, pausing in her
attempt to alphabetize the stack in her lap. "The
station?"

"I took brownies to the guys at work before I
came here." Liz lifted her shoulders in a shrug and
exhaled. "It'd be hard to just suddenly stop baking
and caring for those guys, you know? They're like
family—were. Are." Her lips twisted into a humorless smile. "It's complicated now."

"I wouldn't know." The bitterness in her own
voice startled Marissa, and she hoped Liz wouldn't
notice. She quickly yanked open the A–D file
drawer and pushed an invoice into the proper slot.
Yet she could feel Liz's heavy gaze on her back.

"You weren't involved with Kevin's department?" Surprise filtered through Liz's voice. "I
thought that was one of the best parts of being

a fireman's wife—getting to visit them at work, take the kids to see Daddy, bring snacks."

"I was pregnant and then raising a baby practically alone in another part of the state, so it was a little difficult to do anything extra. Kevin never had family, either." Marissa hesitated. "He didn't really want me to get involved, anyway. Said the guys would just check me out."

Liz chuckled. "Well, you can't fault a man for protecting his wife."

"Something like that." More like Kevin just preferred keeping his professional and personal lives completely separate—a fact that became more obvious when he began choosing work over his family and never letting the two mesh. "Anyway, I guess that was a good thing after the way everything ended. I didn't get attached and was able to move on without even more grief."

"I can only imagine."

"You really miss it, don't you?" Marissa studied her compassionate, generous friend with new eyes. "You were more involved in Ryan's career than I realized."

"I think even more than I realized myself." Liz laughed. She shoved a file folder into the cabinet and shut the drawer with a solid click. "But sometimes the joys of life are a risk. Friendships, working relationships…romantic relationships."

Marissa gripped her stack of papers with tense

knuckles. Liz's overly nonchalant voice would have been a dead giveaway, even if her words weren't. "You're not going to win any subtlety contests, you know."

"Listen, Marissa, I think you and Jacob are the ideal match." Liz's no-nonsense yet encouraging tone tamped the defensiveness rising in Marissa's chest. "I know you have a bad history with firemen, honey, but I didn't say that about risks being worth it for nothing. It's true."

"You think I'm being overly cautious."

"Maybe. But I haven't walked in your shoes." Liz peered over the edge of the desk at Marissa's white sneakers. "Actually, they look pretty comfortable."

Marissa snorted. "I get what you're saying. But if I'm not ready, I'm not ready."

"Just don't listen to yourself say that for longer than it's true."

She frowned. "What do you mean?"

"I'm guessing that's been your mantra for a while." Liz filed the last of her invoices and shrugged. "Maybe you should try convincing yourself you are ready."

"Maybe I could say I'm ready about dating." Marissa nibbled on her lower lip. "But not a fireman again." *Never again.* For some reason, though, the typical rush of emotion didn't accompany the thought. Had she become numb to the idea?

Or was it beginning to take root?

No! Marissa slammed the last file drawer closed. She couldn't even think that. Liz didn't understand the danger. No one did. Like Liz said, they hadn't walked in her shoes. They didn't know how badly her fears ached, how deep the pain ran.

"So you're saying if Jacob had another job, you'd date him?" Liz crossed her arms over her chest and leveled her gaze on Marissa.

"Maybe." The answer felt like a lie, since a resounding *yes* was aching to burst from her heart.

"Every job has danger to it. You can get hurt crossing the street, Marissa. We can't control everything—or really, anything. But a fireman is not guaranteed to get hurt. Look at your dad. He's enjoyed a full career and is near retirement."

Not the best example. Marissa closed her eyes against the headache forming in her skull and sighed. "I hear you, I do. But it's not just about the danger. It's the entire lifestyle. You saw that Jacob had to leave right in the middle of Olivia's party. If a fire doesn't kill him physically, that pager will destroy everything else." Like family. Marriage. Commitments. Marissa swallowed the lump rising in her throat and opened her eyes to find Liz's sympathetic gaze riveted on her. "Thanks for being a good friend. But this isn't an easy fix."

"I don't mean to push. I just want you and my brother-in-law to be happy—whether that's together, or separately." Liz handed Marissa the plate of brownies and grinned. "I think we've burned off sufficient emotional calories. Take the big one."

No kidding. Marissa grabbed the brownie and took a big bite, not even caring about the crumbs that dropped onto her planner. At this point, chocolate stains would be the least of her problems.

It was a good thing they hadn't got called out in the past two hours, because Liz's words still rang so heavy in Jacob's brain he could think of nothing else. He stirred the beef stew simmering on the stove in the station kitchen, grateful it was his night to cook and not Steve's. He could hide in the kitchen and breathe in the savory fumes of the soup until his head cleared. No wonder Marissa carried such reservations about starting a relationship with him. Not only was her father an obvious factor in her hesitations, but she was a widow because of the fire department.

Because of his job.

The hopelessness that had ridden on his shoulders ever since Liz's declaration seemed to suddenly weigh heavier than ever before. Jacob set the wooden spoon on the counter and sighed. Talk about an impasse. Now he wasn't just facing the threat of ticking off the chief by falling for his daughter—he was facing the giant obstacle of convincing Marissa that the career he loved wouldn't leave her alone again.

And that was a promise he wasn't qualified to make.

Jacob wasn't oblivious to the perils of his job, but he didn't dwell on them, either. He was highly trained and certified, and beyond that, his life was in God's hands. Obviously Marissa hadn't come to terms with that yet since her own brush with tragedy. Although he supposed the emotions involved were quite different once a child was in the picture. He thought of Owen's sweet smile and messy hair. He wanted to be there 24-7—for Owen and Marissa both. He wanted to be the boy's hero every day and not just because of his career.

The stew began to boil, mirroring the turmoil in his stomach. Jacob turned down the burners and hollered into the living area, "Soup's on!" He grabbed three bowls from the cabinet and turned, nearly bumping into Captain Walker.

"Here you are. Steve thought you were in the front yard." Captain took the bowls from Jacob so he could grab the spoons and napkins. "I've wanted to talk to you."

"Sorry, Captain. Steve's the one who typically abandons the stove while cooking dinner, not me." Jacob flashed a grin he didn't feel inside and strode past the captain to the worn wooden table in the living area where they ate.

Captain followed with the bowls, which Jacob began placing around the table with a louder clatter than he intended. The captain's eyebrows rose. "Bad day?"

"Just a lot on my mind, sir." Somewhat of an understatement, but Jacob couldn't exactly bear his burden on his superior. Not about this.

"Well, maybe my news will cheer you up." Captain cleared his throat. "What if I told you that you were up for the position of driver?"

Jacob looked up from the table, nearly dropping the bowl in his hands. "What?"

"Don't get too excited." Captain Walker held up both hands in warning. "Obviously there's no room in the budget for a raise right now. But it'd be a promotion in rank, and eventually the pay would increase."

Jacob's pulse hammered in his veins as he struggled to decide if this would be good news or bad. Driver. That meant his focus would be on the truck and pumping water to the firemen, instead of being on the front lines himself. Accepting the position would mean leaving the duties he enjoyed now—actually fighting fires—but it might open a door to ease Marissa's fears. Not to mention once the pay did increase, he could fill the hole in his savings from helping Ryan and Liz.

But he'd be giving up the job he loved, for an indefinite period of time, with no financial benefit. Jacob frowned.

"You'd move to either a different station or a different shift, since we don't need you and Steve both as drivers here. But think about it. The chief wanted me to mention it." Captain laughed as he clapped Jacob on the back. "Seems like he's forgiven you for the water hose incident."

Chief Brady. Jacob's heart plummeted to his stomach, effectively killing his appetite for dinner. Now his career would be in even more jeopardy if the chief discovered his growing feelings for Marissa. The promotion and raise would be a moot point if he got on the chief's bad side. Jacob might be forgiven for spraying him with water, but the chief might not be so easily swayed about his only daughter. Jacob would have to be even more careful about hiding the intentions of his heart—but if he was forced to become more obvious in his pursuit of Marissa, how was that possible?

His head pounded. "Give me some time, Captain. I'll let you know."

"No problem. It's not a done deal, anyway. Just let me know by the end of next week and I'll pass on the word." Captain took his place at the table and frowned. "Aren't you forgetting something?"

Feeling like he was stuck on autopilot, Jacob headed back into the kitchen to bring the pot of stew to the table, his thoughts racing faster than the fire trucks he'd soon be driving.

Or would he?

Chapter Sixteen

Marissa lay in her bed beneath cool sheets, watching the ceiling fan whirl in the dim glow of her alarm clock as Liz's words circled her brain in an equally fast manner. *Sometimes the joys of life are a risk. Friendships, working relationships, romantic relationships.* She adjusted the pillow under her head and sighed. Liz was right. Nothing in life was simple or came freely—she'd learned that particular lesson early on. But that didn't make the pain from going through the hard times any easier to bear. Not with Kevin, not with her dad.

Not with Jacob.

She flipped over on her side with a huff, wishing sleep would come and rob her off these relentless, restless thoughts. Maybe the choices she'd made about avoiding firemen—even her own father—had come with a price tag, but those choices had also kept her and Owen safe. Safe from heartache, safe from pain, safe from grave sites.

Safe from love, her conscience mocked her, and for the first time in a long while, Marissa wondered if the price tag was steeper than she was willing to pay. What if she let her father back into her and Owen's life? Would he even want back in? She'd shut that door physically when she moved across the state with Kevin years ago, but now that she was in Orchid Hill again, there were no more barriers other than the emotional walls she'd constructed. Her mother fit into Owen's life; why couldn't the chief? Would he even be willing to spend his precious time away from the station to be involved?

Or was it simply too late? Memories of Owen as an infant in her dad's arms for the first time flooded her mind. Owen's chubby cheeks and her father's proud grandpa smile. They'd put aside their differences at Owen's birth. What had happened in the years to follow?

And Jacob. Marissa covered her eyes with one hand and groaned. His smile and caring eyes danced before her and she quickly opened her eyes. Yet his image lingered in her exhausted mind. She couldn't escape her feelings for him, any more than she could rewind time and prevent Kevin from going to work that fateful day in December. She'd risked a lot marrying Kevin, knowing the life of a fireman's family was more difficult than most. It seemed crazy to risk it again, after living through her worst nightmare at his funeral.

But trying to deny her growing feelings for Jacob seemed just as impossible. What blessings would she miss by clinging to her resolve to be "safe"? But what heartache would she have to endure if she took the risk?

Her cell suddenly blared from her nightstand, and Marissa jerked upright, tossing the covers back in an attempt to grab the phone before it woke Owen down the hall. Her feet tangled in the sheets and she flopped hard across the bed on her stomach, catching a glimpse of the alarm clock. 1:45 a.m. She snatched the phone, scraping it against the table as her heart drummed in her throat. "Hello?"

"Marissa, it's Jacob." His voice, tighter than a wound coil, simmered through the line, only adding to her anxiety. "I'm sorry to have to wake you."

"Is everything all right? Is Liz okay? Olivia?" Marissa pressed a shaky hand to her forehead as her stomach performed cartwheels, imagining the worst.

"They're fine." Jacob hesitated. "It's your dad. He's on his way to the E.R. with severe chest pains."

Marissa sucked in a deep breath of air that suddenly felt frigid to her lungs, and her cell phone slipped from her fingers onto the bed. Jacob's voice, tiny and muted, continued to sound from the top of the covers but she didn't care. Minutes ago she'd been worried that it was too late for her and her father to ever repair their relationship after all they'd been through.

Now it might be later than she'd thought.

"Where is he?" Marissa's sneakers squeaked against the linoleum floor as she paced in front of the receptionist area. The woman behind the desk, who seemed to be moving much too slowly to work in the E.R., made a few clicks of her computer mouse, her expression unnervingly calm.

"Your father was just brought in, ma'am. He's still being treated."

"But for what? What happened?" Marissa gripped the counter and fought the hysterics rising in her chest. "All I know is chest pains." Severe chest pains, Jacob had said. How severe? How serious? Was she too late?

"That's all they know at this point, too." The receptionist's dark eyes warmed with sympathy. "Maybe you'd like some coffee while you wait? There's a machine just down the hall."

Sympathy, maybe, but she probably also wanted Marissa to get away from her desk before she made her dizzy from the pacing. Marissa could take a hint. But she hesitated to let go of the counter for fear her trembling legs wouldn't support her.

Sudden arms wrapped around her shoulders, and Marissa sensed it was Jacob before he even spoke. "It's okay. He'll be fine."

With a muted cry, Marissa burrowed into his embrace, his warm baritone vibrating through his chest against her ear, his T-shirt soft against her cheek. She clung like a drowning woman as the sobs began to build.

"This way." Jacob eased Marissa away long enough to hook an arm around her waist and guide her away from the E.R. "There's a nicer waiting area down the hall with coffee. Your mom was there before they let her go back with the chief."

"So Mom is with him now?" At Jacob's nod, Marissa took a shaky breath through her tears. No wonder her mom hadn't answered the dozen calls to her cell Marissa had made on the way to the hospital. At least her father wasn't alone, although she couldn't remember a time growing up the chief had been scared. He wasn't afraid of anything.

But this incident had her shaken to the core.

"I volunteered to call you so your mom could hurry back with him once they allowed it," Jacob said as he gestured toward the waiting room chairs. "She was a little rattled, understandably. I don't know if she would have made much sense to you."

Probably for the best. Her mother didn't handle tragedy well, a fact proven about five years ago when Marissa had to make one very hard phone call herself.

"Black coffee okay?" Jacob helped Marissa into the blue plastic chair. "We might be here awhile." He counted loose change in his hand while he waited for her answer.

She nodded numbly, the past and present tumbling over themselves in rampant succession. *Don't go back there, Marissa. Don't do it.*

"I'll make sure the receptionist knows to tell your mother you're out here, okay? I'll be right back." Jacob offered a reassuring smile before practically jogging down the long, fluorescent-lit hallway toward the vending area. For the first time, the writing on the back of his shirt, ORCHID HILL F.D., did nothing to set off her emotions. They were already on overload, and she stared at the letters growing smaller before Jacob turned the corner.

She closed her eyes, head resting against the hard back of the chair, the wooden armrests biting into her forearms, and tried to think positively. Tried to pray. But all she could remember was a similar night of a knock on the door and bad news that rocked her world forever. Scrambling to find a babysitter last minute, just like she'd done tonight. Rushing to the hospital even though she knew it was too late.

She couldn't be too late again. Not when she'd finally had a breakthrough of the dark cynicism surrounding her memories of her dad. *Please, God.* She repeated the mantra over and over.

"Here you go. It's hot." A warm cup was shoved in her hands and Marissa looked up, nearly drowning in the compassion radiating from Jacob's expression. "I brought sugar packets just in case. This stuff is stout."

"Why are you here?" Marissa took a sip, wincing at both the searing of her tongue and the words that tumbled out harsher than she intended. Jacob flinched as he sat down beside her, and she instinctively touched his arm to erase her mistake. "I didn't mean it that way. I'm sorry."

He nodded. "I know. It's the stress talking, I've seen it more often than I'd like." He cradled his steaming cup in his hands and sighed. "I was at the station when I heard the chief had been working late at headquarters, and fell down with pain in his office at the main complex. He was able to dial 911, which obviously alerted us." Jacob shrugged. "I couldn't let you go through this alone. I rode with the chief in the ambulance and made sure your mom was notified before calling you."

"That was thoughtful." Marissa's words came out a whisper and she cleared her throat of the residual emotion that seemed lodged inside. "Thank you."

Jacob met her gaze then, his eyes reflecting their usual warmth and sensitivity. "How's Owen? Did you tell him?"

"No, I didn't want to scare him. On the way to Liz's house I just told him I had to take care of something and would call him in the morning." Marissa sipped her coffee, now a more tolerable heat. "I think he was too sleepy to care."

"I'm sorry about all this. But if it helps, your dad never lost consciousness, which is a great sign. I think if he could have ordered the paramedic around, he would have." Jacob winked.

"Sounds like Dad." Marissa smiled, but it slowly faded as a fresh burst of fear erupted in her stomach. "What if he's not going to be okay? What if he has permanent heart damage? Or can't work anymore?" Tears clogged her eyes and she jammed her palm against the dam threatening to explode. "That alone would kill him if this doesn't." Ironic that she was now concerned her father wouldn't be able to do the very thing she resented his entire life. What was wrong with her?

Jacob set his coffee on the table by the row of chairs and drew Marissa as close as the armrest between them would allow. "It's okay," he whispered against her hair. "God hasn't forgotten your father. Or you."

"You say that so confidently." Marissa sniffed and pulled away, embarrassment at her lack of composure heating her face. She couldn't even think about how she must look—tearstained cheeks, no makeup, sloppy ponytail fresh from bed. She did a double take at her clothes to make sure she'd actually thrown on something decent before running out of the house, relieved to see her favorite football team sweatshirt and faded jeans.

"I am confident," Jacob answered. He hesitated, as if not sure how much to say or how much physical space to give her. He finally slid back into his chair, turning slightly to face her and crossing his ankles. "Pastor Rob makes that abundantly clear each Sunday from Bible passages. God's word never lies."

Marissa plucked at the loose strands of fabric covering the hole in her jeans. "It's easier to believe that more at certain times than others."

"Others meaning in an E.R.?"

She swallowed. "Or at a grave site."

Jacob's heart welled with mixed emotion— compassion, frustration and a tightening in his chest he could only label love. *God, I want to fix this, and I can't.* He couldn't erase the past, and at the moment, his hands were tied regarding a future with Marissa, too. But he had the present, and if all he could do was offer Marissa a comforting shoulder now, he'd do it.

Even if it ripped apart his insides.

"Is this bringing back bad memories?" He kept his voice low, not willing to let the older man who settled into a chair across from them in on their sensitive conversation.

"A few." Marissa rubbed the length of her face with her hand. Jacob's eyes felt as bloodshot as hers looked, and he took another sip of coffee.

"I get the feeling you and your father have never been…close." Jacob darted a sideways glance her direction, hoping he hadn't overstepped his boundaries.

Marissa shrugged. "That's probably the understatement of the century."

"What happened?"

The simple question unleashed a torrent of words from Marissa, each sentence spilling over the other in a waterfall of pain and regret. Missed recitals. Late nights. Too many gruff words, not enough affection. "He was never there." She sniffed as she summed up the fast-forward account of her childhood. "And then I pushed him away in defense." She shook her head. "And if I'm completely honest, also as punishment."

"Understandable. You were hurting." Jacob

touched her hand, grateful she didn't pull away. "You've been through a lot in your life, Marissa. More than I could imagine. Don't let the guilt trips beat you up now." Jacob hated that his suspicions had been right. No wonder Marissa hated the idea of getting involved with a fireman. Not only had her husband died on the job, but her experience within the family of a fireman had also been negative. She'd already had two strong strikes against the career—there was no way she'd be interested in a third with him. The thought brought equal measures of understanding and grief.

"There was so much I should have done differently." She stared aimlessly toward the magazines spread on the table before them, their pages tattered and worn from too many fingers anxiously flipping through. Tired. Worn. He could relate.

Jacob threaded his fingers through Marissa's, hope rising as she gripped his hand tighter. "I wish I could help." *I wish I could find a solution. I wish I could make this work.* But he couldn't say that. Not without taking advantage of her emotions.

"You are helping." She finally looked up, an exhausted but grateful smile turning her lips. "If it weren't for you, I'd be sitting here alone." Then she leaned sideways and rested her head on his shoulder.

Jacob tilted his head to subtly breathe in the sweet aroma of her hair. He never wanted her to be alone again. But this wasn't exactly the time or place to make such a declaration—not with her father's life in jeopardy, and not with his own career on the line. He knew better than to rush important moments in the face of potential tragedy, and didn't want either of them to say anything they'd regret later.

But the longer she nestled against his arm, the more he realized he'd regret not saying something a whole lot more.

He sat up, easing her away to meet his gaze. His heart thundered a storm in his chest and his blood raced. This was probably one of the dumbest things he'd ever do, but he had to say what he felt. He swallowed hard, his tongue thick with anxiety. "Marissa, I—"

"Marissa!" Her mother stepped into the waiting room, dark circles under her eyes, arms crossed over her thin body. A tired smile lit her face, chasing away the shadows of fear. "I'm so glad you made it."

Marissa jumped up, pulling her hand from Jacob and rushing to meet her mother near the door. "How is he?"

"Your father is going to be fine. It's angina, not a heart attack." Mrs. Brady clenched Marissa in a tight hug. "The doctors said he has high blood pressure from stress. He's got to make some changes, but the danger is past."

With a happy cry, Marissa hugged her mother back. Jacob looked away from the private moment, grateful the woman he loved would get another chance to make things right.

And wondering if he'd ever get the chance to do the same.

Chapter Seventeen

Despite his bulk filling the hospital bed, Marissa had never seen her father look so old. Monitors beeped as she approached his bed, her heart in her throat and her hands shaky.

Her mother gently prodded her back. "Go on. He's awake."

Marissa took a few steps nearer and gingerly reached out to the chief's hand. He opened his eyes and with some effort, rolled his head to meet her gaze. His hand tightened around hers and fresh tears filled her eyes. "You really shouldn't scare us like this, Dad. It's not professional." She tried to smile around the lingering fear.

The chief snorted his agreement as he shifted positions beneath the thin green blanket. "You can say that again. My men don't need a weak example."

"That's ridiculous and you know it." Marissa's

fear dissipated and she gripped his hand tighter. "You're the strongest person I know."

Her dad's eyes filled with a rush of emotion and he swallowed, his Adam's apple bobbing in his throat. "Back at ya, kid."

Marissa's throat burned with unshed tears. She clutched her dad's hand, praying she wasn't about to wake up and find this had all been a dream. To be so near reconciliation and to find out it wasn't real would be nothing short of a nightmare.

Marissa's mom scooted past Marissa to settle into the chair by the chief's bedside, jolting Marissa out of her thoughts. "Strong or not, we're about to make some changes around here. All of us." She dipped her head in Marissa's direction before turning her gaze back on her husband. "You've been too stressed lately and trying to hide it. No more of that—and no more late nights at the office with a pizza in one hand and a burger in the other."

The chief's thick brows knitted over his eyes, but she lifted her chin before he could reply. "I learned a few tricks about stubborn over the years, and I intend to keep you around to learn some more." Her gaze gentled and they shared a smile.

Marissa cleared her throat, unsure how to handle affection between her family. This was new. Wonderful, but new. She eased her hand out of her dad's grip and leaned against the wall, her arms crossed over her chest. She wished Jacob had come inside with them instead of waiting in the hallway. He'd wanted to give them privacy. So why did it seem like he should be there?

Because he's already a part of your heart.

Marissa forced the truth aside, unable to handle any more strong emotions that hour. "When do you get to go home?"

The chief rolled his eyes, his typical demeanor returning. "Not soon enough. They still want to run some tests as a precaution and keep me here at least one more night. Seems like overkill to me."

The word *kill* shuddered through Marissa's body. She couldn't stand here now that the immediate danger was past and not say what she'd longed to have the chance to just minutes ago. She opened her mouth, then hesitated. "Dad?" She glanced at her mom, who looked up, then quickly grabbed a magazine, as if afraid to even hope for the coming conversation.

"What?" the chief fairly barked.

"I'm...sorry." The words floated from her lips, barely louder than a whisper, and Marissa tried again, louder. "I'm sorry for—everything. The last few years, especially. I mean—"

The chief held up one hand to stop the embarrassing rush of words that couldn't seem to join together the way she intended. "Me, too." He held out his hand and Marissa rushed to grab it, joy pushing away the residual fear in her heart as she clung to his arm.

"I haven't been honest with you," her father said, the lines of his brow creasing as he frowned. "I've wanted you off the festival project not just because of the arson fires but because I've been suppressing guilt. Your being involved just drudged up everything I kept fighting to keep down."

Marissa tilted her head. "What do you mean? What guilt?"

"I should have been able to stop the council from their decision about the layoffs. I let my boys down." A muscle in her father's jaw twitched and he looked away, blinking rapidly. "And I let the stress of it all put me in here, where it was almost too late."

"Dad, it wasn't your fault."

He shrugged, finally meeting her gaze once again. "It is what it is. Maybe I should have spoken up more, not been afraid for my own position. Maybe it wouldn't have helped, anyway. But now I'll never know." He drew a deep breath. "But I was wrong to take my frustrations out on you for your doing a good deed. You've done the right thing by these men. I wish I could say the same."

Hope swelled in Marissa's chest. "It's not too late to get involved. I'm sure the families would like to see you at the festival this weekend—if you're out of here, that is."

The chief tugged his hand free and rubbed his chin, chuckling. "Oh, I will be."

"If the doctor says it's all right, of course." Marissa's mom leveled a glare at her husband, though the gesture still spoke of love.

Watching the two of them interact as only an old married couple could increased her desire to see Jacob. Marissa edged toward the door. "I'm going to, uh, go get something from the vending machine." She glanced at her mom, who shot her a knowing look with a quirk of her lips. "Want anything?"

"Two chocolate bars," the chief joked.

"Nothing for either of us, thanks." Marissa's mom shot another warning glance. "We'll be here when you get back." When she looked at Marissa, her eyes softened. "And you tell Jacob we'd like to see him before he leaves. I think your father has something to tell him."

Marissa agreed and slipped outside, shutting the door behind her with a soft click. She leaned against it and briefly closed her eyes, breathing a silent prayer of thanks to God for a second chance.

"Hey, there. Everything all right?" At the sound of Jacob's voice, Marissa opened her eyes, meeting his gaze to find all her hopes and fears for the future together in one place.

If only second chances could come more often. "He's doing great. Ornery as usual." She smiled, relief filling her chest as the last of her anxiety melted away. Leftover adrenaline still shook her legs. "I better get going before Owen wakes up and gets even more confused with me gone. My parents want to see you before you go, though."

"I'll walk you to the parking lot and come back up." Jacob tucked her hand into the crook of his arm as they headed down the hall toward the elevators. "Don't want to keep the little man waiting."

Marissa leaned against Jacob as they rode down, grateful for his strength. Her legs felt like overcooked spaghetti noodles. She drew a steadying breath as the doors opened onto the first level. "Amazing how a few minutes can change everything, huh?"

"It doesn't take long for life to become different. I'd imagine you know that better than anyone." He hesitated as they strolled through the lobby. "Marissa, there's something I know that I don't think you know I know."

"Blame the fact that it's 4:00 a.m., but I have no idea what you just said." Marissa laughed and stopped in front of the glass sliding doors. "What's going on?"

He tugged her outside, away from the receptionist and the E.R. patients waiting in the lobby, and paused beside the concrete column by the entrance. "This might not be the best time, but with the festival coming up, I don't want anything between us at work and I feel like I'm keeping a secret."

"What secret?" Marissa frowned, a fresh wave of nerves wrapping around her middle. She crossed her arms, hoping this wasn't another example of life changing in a moment. The security light above their heads buzzed, deafening in the silence as she waited.

"I didn't know before, but I do now." Jacob raked his fingers through his already mussed hair. "I know your late husband was a fireman." He looked down, then in her eyes. "I sort of pried it out of Liz."

Marissa nodded slowly, pulling in her lower lip. She wasn't sure if his knowing the details of her former life made her feel annoyed or relieved. She exhaled slowly. "It wasn't really a secret. Just not something I broadcasted." She snorted. "I guess Liz did that enough for the both of us."

"Don't be upset with her, it really wasn't her fault." Jacob sighed. "I just could tell there was more to your story and I couldn't handle not knowing what it was." He gingerly reached out and brushed a strand of hair behind her ears. "I'm sorry I wasn't more understanding before. If I had known he died in the line of duty, I wouldn't have been so pushy about...well, about us."

Marissa shivered at his touch, tilting her head to catch the warmth of his hand on her cheek. A brisk wind sent discarded flower petals from the nearby beds rushing past their feet, and Marissa followed the rejected petals with her eyes as they danced across the parking lot. Once beautiful and full of life, now on their way to being crushed by a passing car or stomped underfoot.

She pulled away, and Jacob's arm fell limply to his side. "I'm not upset with Liz. Or with you." She shrugged, avoiding the compassion brewing in his eyes. "I just don't want pity."

Jacob took a step closer to her. The breeze caressed his hair, the dark strands drawing attention to his intense blue gaze. "I would never insult you with pity, Marissa."

She tried not to miss his warmth and huddled into her sweatshirt in a vain effort to escape the wind, edging backward two steps to his one. "I don't know what you want from me."

"Yes, you do." His voice was low, dangerous to her heart and the building emotion congealing in her throat. He didn't touch her, but his proximity burned her body like a brand.

Because he's already a part of your heart. Her own thoughts flickered through her mind like an undeniable record on repeat. She made the mistake of darting a glance to his lips, and a spark jolted through her stomach. Jacob pressed forward, his hand cupping her neck and halting her escape. "Marissa, I want you. I want to be an 'us.' I want to be more than a begrudged friend to your son. I want to be your own personal hero." He inhaled sharply. "And I really want to kiss you."

She opened her mouth, unsure if she would argue or agree, but Jacob's lips were on hers before she could decide. He kissed her gently, then with more fervor, pulling her close until she snuggled into his embrace like a missing puzzle piece. She kissed him back, all the fear and relief and gratitude of the night flowing through her body as she wrapped her arms around his neck.

Jacob abruptly stepped back, ending the kiss. He held her away by the shoulders, head ducked low as he caught his breath. When he met her gaze, electricity shot from his eyes into her own. "I'm sorry, I shouldn't have taken advantage of you like that. I know you're emotional tonight, and—"

Heart racing as reality once more claimed her like gravity, Marissa jerked away and finished his sentence. "And this isn't going to happen." Tears filling her eyes, she attempted to pull her car keys from her pocket. Disappointment and longing racked her senses, and she fumbled with the ring before finding the right key. She thought if she could just make it through the festival, she'd be free of Jacob's proximity and be able to think of him as just a family member of her new friend. But after his kiss, after getting a tangible knowledge of his feelings for her and her own for him, that would be impossible. He'd ruined her master plan, and it was her own fault for allowing him too close.

"Why not?" Hope and desperation mingled in Jacob's eyes. "I don't care about the risk, Marissa. I don't even care about my job anymore. I care about you." He reached for her again and she held up both hands in defense. "Give me one good reason, Marissa. Just one."

One? There were twelve, spelled out in the bold letters on the back of his T-shirt. "I just can't. I can't do this again." Fingers clenched around her keys, Marissa backpedaled through the nearly deserted lot, hoping to make it to her car before bursting into tears. "But thanks for being here tonight." Her voice caught and she choked out her next words. "Thanks for being honest."

She turned then to avoid the pain stabbing her insides at his dejected expression, and raced for the security of her car before he could respond. Her pulse hammered in time to her racing feet. *And thanks for breaking my heart.*

* * *

Jacob jabbed the elevator button with his thumb as if hoping it'd break into a thousand pieces. His heart still thumped so loudly the receptionist must have thought he needed an EKG. Marissa's rejection echoed through his body like a war drum, and blood rushed in his ears. What had just happened? His lips still tingled from her kiss, and his hands shook like he was back in junior high with a crush. He stabbed the elevator button again in a futile effort to convince the mechanisms to work faster.

The doors opened with a polite ding, and he felt like punching that, too. Instead, he ducked his head and drew a calming breath as the elevator ushered him back to Chief Brady's room. He was a man on a mission—more like a kamikaze mission, but he couldn't handle it anymore. He had to know the truth, had to know what his obstacles were if he had any hope of getting around them.

Starting with the biggest.

Jacob knocked twice on the cracked door to room 313. "It's Jacob Greene."

"Come on in."

Mrs. Brady smiled from the bedside chair as Jacob eased his way inside, closing the door behind him. "He's awake. I can't vouch for his mood, however." She winked.

"How you feeling, sir?" Jacob paused by the

chief's bed, glad the hefty man's coloring was better than it had been earlier that night.

"Like a piñata." The chief snorted as he adjusted the bed into a sitting position. "Never did like those things."

"You've been through a lot of poking and prodding." Jacob hung back from the bed, offering a respectful distance as he leaned casually against the adjacent wall. "But you don't look worse for the wear."

"I appreciate the lie."

Jacob chuckled, and the chief's eyes lit with rarely seen humor before darkening into a serious expression.

"You didn't have to stand by me tonight the way you did. But you took charge, and that's commendable." He nodded briskly. "So, thank you."

"I wouldn't have even considered anything different, sir. You're the chief." Jacob hesitated, then blurted the truth before he could change his mind. "And you're also the father of the woman I love."

The chief blanched, and Mrs. Brady gasped, the magazine she'd been flipping through falling from her fingers. "Come again?"

"I don't mean to shock you, sir, you've been through enough tonight." Jacob shrugged. "But I've struggled with this for weeks and I respect you enough to tell you the truth. At first I was afraid for my job. I know what happened with the fireman you shipped to Baton Rouge."

The chief snorted and Mrs. Brady shot him a glare. "You did what?"

"Let the boy finish speaking." The chief waved her off.

Jacob darted a glance between the two of them before cautiously continuing. "My brother was one of the men laid off this past round, and I've been helping them financially. I couldn't afford to risk my job, especially now that I'm up for the promotion." He hesitated, then met the chief's gaze full on. "But with all due respect, sir, I love your daughter too much to be that concerned anymore."

Mrs. Brady's jaw gaped and the chief nodded to himself, his throat bobbing several times before he spoke. "A week ago, even two days ago, I'd have told you to keep your distance. My little girl's been through enough in her short life, and me and her, well—" He coughed loudly. "We're just now finding our footing again. But after tonight…"

Jacob's stomach tightened as he waited for the end of the chief's sentence. Hope and fear mingled in a knot he didn't dare yet attempt to untangle.

"After tonight, I see the man you are." The corners of the chief's lips twisted into a wry smile. "Your heart's right there on your sleeve, son. I didn't ever want to be one of those sops who had a brush with the grim reaper and turned all soft, but to be honest, I can't imagine a better man for my daughter."

Joy burst in Jacob's heart and he straightened in surprise, elation threatening to send him right out of his boots. "Thank you, sir. You won't be sorry."

"Now if you tell anyone I said that I'll deny it." Chief shot him a warning look, his bloodshot eyes drooping as he settled back against his pillow. "But the way I see it, if you can change Marissa's stubborn mind about firemen, you deserve her."

Jacob wasn't sure if anyone could do that. But one thing was certain—he'd gladly give it a fair fight. "I appreciate it, sir. I'll do my best." He took a few steps toward the door, eager to leave before the chief could change his mind and before Jacob could beat himself up for taking such a risk with his boss in a hospital bed. "I'll leave now so you can sleep."

"By the way, that promotion to driver is yours if you want it—regardless of what happens with you and Marissa. I don't run my department that way." The chief glanced at his wife's pursed lips and then rolled his eyes. "At least, not anymore."

Jacob smiled. "Yes, sir." He opened the door, disbelief blurring his vision. His main obstacle to Marissa was removed. Well, not the main one, but the most intimidating one, to be sure. He'd have

to think about the promotion opportunity further.
But there was time for that.

"Jacob?" the chief called.

He turned in the hallway. "Sir?"

Chief offered a tired grin. "Good luck."

Chapter Eighteen

Early morning sunshine peeked through the sheer curtains, sending thin streams of light onto Liz's couch where Marissa sat, cradling a mug of tea between both hands. She leaned over the cup, inhaling the aromatic steam, and groaned. "I can't believe I was up all night. I haven't done that since Owen was teething."

"Maybe the caffeine will help." Liz yawned, leaning back against the cushions where she sat beside Marissa. "If not, you can always hit up a Starbucks on the way home."

"Owen was sleeping so soundly, I couldn't bear to wake him up and confuse him even further." Marissa shot her friend a weary but grateful smile. "Thanks again for your help. I don't know what I would have done without you last night." Her smile faded as the memories fought for reign in her exhausted mind. "Or without Jacob."

Liz curled her legs underneath her on the couch and leaned forward, a gleam of interest replacing the sheen of exhaustion in her eyes. "He has his heroic moments, even outside of the fire department, doesn't he?"

"He was a rock." Marissa swallowed the knot in her throat. "And I hurt him." She filled Liz in on the details of their parting just a few hours earlier. "I can't believe I was so harsh. But that kiss…" She briefly closed her eyes. "It terrified me."

"Because it showed you your feelings?" Liz asked.

Marissa slowly shook her head. "Because it proved what I already knew."

"Don't leave a girl hanging." Liz sipped from her own mug of tea. "What'd you know?"

Marissa took a deep breath, the truth hovering on her lips, unable to be denied. "That I love him."

Liz squealed, her tea sloshing dangerously in the cup as she jerked forward and set the mug on a coaster on the coffee table. "I told you!" She cleared her throat in a pathetic attempt to regain her composure. "I mean, I'm glad you finally see it."

Marissa plucked at a loose thread in the afghan covering her lap. "Seeing my dad in a hospital bed…" Her voice broke off and she sniffed. "Everything you've told me, everything I've heard at church recently and known my entire life but was never able to put into practice was suddenly right in front of me. I had a choice to make."

Liz nodded for her to go on.

"I could choose to stay safe and block myself off from the love of my father, because of our past." Marissa rolled in her lower lip, thinking. "Or I could embrace it and start life again. He was given a second chance, and I'd like to think I was, too, in a different way." She smiled as a wistful melancholy settled over her weary shoulders. "And after Jacob kissed me, I was staring at the same choice but in Technicolor."

"What did you choose?" Liz's brow furrowed, as if afraid she already knew the answer. "You just said you hurt Jacob. I'm guessing that means you're still not ready?"

"My heart says one thing, my head says another." Marissa stared out the picture window behind the couch at Liz's backyard stirring to life. A baby bird took a dip in the concrete bath next to the flower beds, and a frog hopped from one stepping stone to another toward the storage shed. Marissa's father was still in a hospital bed, and the man she'd grown to love despite every attempt not to thought she despised him. Yet the world continued to revolve while she sat on Liz's couch, dizzy from the revelations of the past twenty-four hours.

Liz's soft voice broke the silence. "Then it sounds

like you need to decide once and for all who you're going to listen to."

"After this incident with my father, I've decided I can't listen to either my heart or my head. I need to ask for God's direction, like I used to do before I was so burned." The words nearly stuck in Marissa's throat but she struggled to get them out, determined to take positive steps toward a new future—one full of life, not of fear. "But after tonight I don't know if Jacob will forgive me. He poured out his heart, and I practically stomped on it and ran away."

"He'll forgive you. Jacob can't hold grudges for long." Liz picked up her mug and took another sip.

Marissa's fingers worried the blanket threads. "I don't know, Liz. You didn't see his face." Or his eyes. That haunted expression of regret and heartache. Jacob had been her knight in shining armor the entire night, going above and beyond the call of duty for her dad and for her, and she'd reacted by shoving his feelings back in his face and storming away. How heartless could she be? It was obvious how much he risked for her—and yet she gave nothing in return other than rejection.

Again.

"I'm sure he'll understand. You've had an emotional night." Liz shifted positions on the couch, uncrossing her legs and leaning forward to punctuate her statement. "But you can find a way to show him how you feel. Maybe through something at the festival?"

"Maybe." Marissa sighed. "But the other issue is my father. Even though it's been my own fear that's kept Jacob at a distance, Jacob said all along my dad wouldn't like the idea of us together. He's right." She shook her head. "I can't allow Jacob to ruin his career and let you guys down because of me. It isn't right."

"Listen to me." Liz grabbed Marissa's hand and squeezed it between her own. "The only thing that would let me down now is if you and Jacob sacrificed any more than you already have. It's not Jacob's job to provide for my family. We've gratefully accepted his help, but it's ultimately God's job to take care of our needs. I'm trusting Him for that—not Jacob." Liz smiled and released Marissa's hand. "So take me and Ryan and Olivia out of the equation. This needs to be a threefold decision." She pointed to Marissa and ticked off on her fingers. "You, Jacob and God. That's it."

Liz was right. If Marissa was truly going to put her fears behind her and allow a fresh start for her and her dad, and for her and Jacob, she was going to have to go all out. Either God was leading her down these paths, or He wasn't. Her heart assured her He was—and that meant He would eventually take care of the details.

If only she'd step back out of the way long enough to let Him.

* * *

Jacob stifled a yawn, his long night at the hospital shading his thoughts with scribbles of gray dejection. He'd come home and napped for a few hours, but his talk a few hours ago with the chief echoed in his mind and wouldn't allow his brain to slow down for deep sleep, despite the lingering fatigue. He threw open the storage shed door and grabbed his Weed Eater, determined to be productive if nothing else. The festival was tomorrow, and while the yard was already in good shape, it could stand another trim.

He roared the motor and welcomed the buzz interrupting the drone of his own thoughts as he mowed around the edge of the shed, the noon sun beating down on his shoulders and neck. The crew of vendors and volunteers would be arriving that evening to set up their booths for the big day, and the festival would start at ten o'clock sharp the next morning. He'd get to see Marissa—that is, if she wasn't too busy running around like a headless chicken all day—and then what? After the festival, he'd have no reason to see Marissa on a daily basis, unless he purposefully risked his heart a second—no, third—time and continued to pursue her while she dodged his every advance. He'd thought obtaining the chief's blessing would put things in motion, but if Marissa was determined never to get involved with a fireman, what choices did he really have? Would knowing she had her father's blessing even matter? And where did Owen come into play?

He finished trimming around the shed and moved toward the house, pausing to whack a stubborn patch of weeds at the end of his driveway. Stubborn, just like Marissa. But also just like himself. If he really loved her, he wouldn't stop trying to win her, regardless of how insane it might seem. Because no matter how crazy it was to continue to throw his heart out there for a beating, he was crazier about Marissa. He wouldn't give up—couldn't. But without a change, his efforts could easily stay in vain. What choices did he have?

Other than quitting his job.

Jacob pulled up the Weed Eater, not wanting to risk whacking the side of his house and damaging the machine as the ugly thought invaded his mind. It seemed to be the only answer to calm Marissa's fears, but how could he give up his retirement and benefits? Give up being able to help his family in need? Firefighting was all he knew. He didn't have a degree to fall back on, had no other means of providing besides his lawn business, and that wasn't nearly enough income alone.

He could take the promotion to driver, and advance his career. But without the promise of extra pay, he'd rather stay where he was, in the midst of his passion—firefighting. The career of a driver would be different. He'd only be doing the duties he loved now if the station was understaffed or in the middle of a big emergency. However, if Jacob ever hoped to make it to Captain, he'd have to go through the process.

And if he went through it now, Marissa might be willing to go through it with him.

His cell vibrated in his pocket, interrupting the flow of thoughts, and he turned off the Weed Eater before yanking the phone from his pocket. "Hello?"

"Jacob? It's Marissa." Her timid voice sent tremors through his body and he dropped the Weed Eater on the ground.

"Are you all right? How's your dad?" Now it was his turn to panic from the other end of a phone line. A fresh burst of sympathy wafted through him at what she must have felt when he called her the night before.

"He's getting to come home tonight if all goes well today with the remaining tests."

Jacob's shoulders slumped and he exhaled with relief. *Thank You, Lord.* He picked up the Weed Eater and switched his phone to his other ear as he began to cart the machine back to the shed. "That's good news. I'm glad you called." He swallowed the knot in his throat, hating the awkward silence pulsing through the connection. Had he ruined things between them forever with his kiss? That hadn't been his intention. But the memory of her lips still burned.

"There's more." Marissa's voice lifted in excitement. "They caught the arsonist. Dad got a call earlier at the hospital with the good news. It wasn't a family member or a fireman like I feared." She snorted a humorless laugh. "I feel ridiculous now for ever suspecting, but my dad's paranoia was contagious."

Gratitude flooded Jacob's body as he shut the shed door. He knew it couldn't have been any of his friends or coworkers, but to have their names cleared was a relief. "So who was it?"

"Some local jerk seizing an opportunity for publicity." Marissa's tone hardened. "According to the detective who called my dad, this guy just wanted his fifteen minutes of fame and knew the public would assume it was related to the layoffs. Some people are so sick."

"It's an ugly world," Jacob agreed, locking the barn door. "But I'm glad our men are off the proverbial hook."

"Me, too." Marissa hesitated. "Dad is actually looking forward to the festival tomorrow. I can't believe how much has changed, literally overnight." A smile lit her voice. "God is good."

Jacob stopped short, nearly tripping over the ramp leading into his shed. "I'm glad you're realizing that again." Although *glad* didn't even begin to touch his level of joy. But exactly how much had changed? If Marissa was finally in the position to let go of her past and embrace her faith again, maybe her calloused heart would soften toward him, too. Maybe if she knew her father wasn't an issue between them anymore, they could take a step forward. Hope sprung in Jacob's chest and his pulse began to beat a hard rhythm in his veins. It was definitely worth a shot. "Marissa, I need to tell you something. Last night after you left, I talked to—"

Something clicked from Marissa's end of the line.

"Uh-oh. My mom is beeping in on the other line. I better take this, might be about Dad again. I'll see you tomorrow at the festival. Tell the volunteers tonight if they need anything to call my cell, okay? I'm going to be finishing up some stuff from home but I can come out if there's a dire need."

"All right, but Marissa—"

But she had already disconnected. Jacob slowly slid his cell into his pocket, leaning back against the side of the shed and resting his head against the rough wood. He'd have to wait until the festival or maybe even afterward to talk to her. And yet again, he'd be taking a huge risk that it would do any good. What if Marissa knew they had her father's blessing and didn't care? What if she was truly never able to get past his career? What if even his sacrifice of switching jobs to become a driver didn't matter?

What if she rejected him once and for all?

Jacob's throat closed at the idea of never getting to see Marissa again, never getting to watch the sunlight turn her hair to the color of honey, never getting to tease Owen or slap him a high five. He wanted so much more than that. He wanted to eat dinner with the two of them every night, wanted to push the shopping cart for Marissa through the grocery store, wanted to check the oil in her car and hound her for not going to get her tires rotated on time. All the things good husbands did.

God, I know this situation is in Your timing, but this is getting really hard. He couldn't sit still another minute, not with the urgency to capture Marissa's heart for his own strumming through his veins. But what could he do? Pushing her before she was ready wasn't the answer—he'd proven that much last night with his impromptu kiss. Jacob released a tight breath and cast a cursory glance around his yard, frustration gripping his spirit and refusing release.

Maybe one more round with the Weed Eater wouldn't hurt.

Chapter Nineteen

Dozens of red-and-white-striped tents dotted Jacob's yard, sunshine slipping off their canvas roofs and painting the pristine yard with stripes of amber. At least one hundred people milled the manicured grounds, snacking on giant corn dogs and trying their hand at the midway games lining the edges of the roped-off gravel drive. Several children bent over their chalk squares on the road, away from the parking area, scribbling designs onto the warm pavement and giggling as they traded colors. To Marissa's right, one particularly brave church member sat atop a collapsible seat in the dunking tank. To her left, another courageous volunteer balanced atop stilts.

So far, so good. Marissa surveyed the scene before her with a mixture of relief and anxiety, fingers itching to clutch her ever-present planner. But Liz had insisted Marissa stop working and enjoy herself now the carnival was finally here, going as far as to toss the planner into the glove box in Marissa's car. "If you forgot something, it's too late now anyway," was Liz's not-so-reassuring but logical explanation. "So eat cotton candy and have fun with Owen."

The order wasn't that hard to follow. Marissa pulled a tuft of sticky blue candy from her cone and let the puffed sugar dissolve in her mouth as Owen attempted to knock over a pyramid of pins with a plastic ball. His first throw missed, and he frowned as the worker retrieved the ball. "It's okay, buddy. Try again," she urged. Owen nodded, concentrating so hard his tongue peeked between the center of his lips.

CRASH! The pins toppled to the ground and Owen jumped up and down with excitement. "I did it!"

"Good job, Owen!" Marissa slapped her son a high five before he raced to retrieve his prize—a small stuffed alligator.

"Here, Mom." Owen tossed the animal to her and she fumbled to catch it without getting the cotton candy stuck to its green fur. "I need both hands to play again."

Marissa couldn't help but smile as Owen handed the worker another red ticket. Logical and determined, that was her son. How much of that did she pass down to him, honestly? And how much was built in from Kevin's genes? There were plenty of qualities she hoped he inherited from his dad.

But there were plenty she'd love for him to learn from someone else. Marissa's eyes darted once again to Jacob, drawn like a magnet as they'd been most of the morning. Jacob was under a tent across the yard, helping a group of young children with their blooming cacti. The sight brought the memory of their time together at the Boardwalk to the forefront of her mind. Marissa briefly closed her eyes, allowing the memory to sweep her away. Jacob, his hair catching the breeze from the river and eyes sparkling as he looked down at her. Jacob, goofing off in the party supply store with the princess paraphernalia. Jacob, sharing the honesty of his hero heart as he assured Marissa every woman needed to be a princess for a day. Past circumstances had taught her to fear heroes, not seek them out. But somewhere along the way, Jacob had changed that mindset. And she had the feeling it had started the very second he popped the tire off her SUV over a month ago.

Marissa opened her eyes in time to find Jacob staring at her from under the striped tent. He lifted his hand in a hesitant wave, and she waved back. They really needed to talk. She couldn't just pull him aside in the midst of the festival chaos and have a heart-to-heart conversation. What if Liz was wrong and he couldn't forgive her? What if it ended badly? She'd have nowhere to go to nurse her broken emotions or hide the inevitable rash of tears. No, she needed something more subtle, but something Jacob would understand. How could she show him her change of heart without risking public humiliation?

"Mom, I want to get my face painted before we do our chalk square, okay?" Owen tugged at her arm, yanking her back to reality. "Come on!"

Chalk squares. That was another issue of the day. She had no idea what to draw in her and Owen's square, and he'd already asked her twice. She couldn't put it off any longer. Maybe she'd just let him pick. It'd been given to them free, anyway, so who cared if the picture didn't turn out to be a timeless keepsake?

Owen fairly yanked Marissa across the yard to the face painting tables set up by the popcorn stand. "Look, they have fire trucks!" He pointed to the easel of options to pick from, and Marissa bit back an automatic groan. Always a fire truck. Could she never escape it?

Then it hit her. A fire truck. Chalk square. Jacob. Her heart raced with excitement. "Owen, I have an idea!" Now it was Marissa's turn to grab her son's hand and tug him away. "We'll do this next. Let's do our chalk box first, okay, buddy?"

Owen surprisingly put up little protest, and

Marissa knelt beside him on the pavement, the road warming her knees through her jeans, and handed him the sticks of chalk the artist had given them. Red, yellow and white. Perfect. "Here. Draw a fire truck."

Owen sat up straight and flipped his hair out of his eyes. Doubt colored his expression. "Are you sure, Mom? You seem tired of those lately."

Guilt pressed against her shoulders and Marissa drew a deep breath against the weight. "I've never been surer of anything in my life." Time for some changes, including her tolerance of the things that interested her son. *Forgive me, Lord.* The guilt lifted away and she handed Owen the red. "Draw."

Owen grinned and began to sketch a crude fire truck in their square. While he worked, Marissa drew a stick figure of a blonde woman beside it and a stick man beside her. There was just enough room between them for a little stick boy. She finished at the same time as Owen, and she watched him carefully as he examined their completed square.

"That's me." He pointed to the little boy wearing a fireman's hat. "And that's you." He pointed to the stick lady with the blond hair. "But who's that guy?" Owen searched Marissa's eyes, his grin fading as confusion replaced his excitement.

A knot centered in Marissa's throat, and she swallowed. Despite her newfound love for Jacob, if Owen didn't want him in the picture, she couldn't allow it. "That's your fireman friend, Mr. Jacob." She pointed to the white stick man, careful not to smudge the drawing. "I thought maybe it was time for him to start hanging out with us more."

Owen tilted his head, his gaze riveted to the picture as he thought.

Marissa held her breath. "Would that be okay with you?"

"Yeah, that'd be cool. It'd make you happy, right?"

Marissa nodded, unable to speak past the lump in her throat that was now twice as big as before. "It really would."

"I think Dad would be happy that you were happy again."

Tears filled Marissa's eyes and she squeezed Owen into a tight hug. "I think you're right, buddy."

Where was Marissa? Jacob had looked everywhere, short of stooping to peek under the tablecloths of the bake sale booth. He stood on his tiptoes in an effort to see over the crowds lingering at various booths, but to no effect. With a sigh, Jacob handed a red ticket to the popcorn vendor and grabbed a handful of the crunchy corn from the paper bag. He hadn't been able to talk with

Marissa all day, just as he'd feared. But if he kept his feelings to himself one more minute, he feared he'd burst like that little kid's purple balloon just moments ago.

"Jacob." A firm voice sounded from behind, and Jacob turned to see Chief Brady in full uniform, resting his weight on a cane. Mrs. Brady hovered close to his side.

"Sir, it's good to see you out and about." Jacob held out his non-buttery hand, and they shook.

"He was determined to leave that place, regardless." Mrs. Brady swatted his arm. "Although the nurse did win the war about the wheelchair."

"Ridiculous policy," Chief grumbled. "I can walk out of a hospital just fine." He tapped his cane on the hard-packed ground for emphasis.

Jacob smiled. "I'm glad you made it, cane or no cane."

"Enough of the small talk. You know why I'm really here." Chief glanced around as if searching for someone. "What happened with Marissa? Did she shoot you down yet?" The comment earned him another swat from Mrs. Brady.

"No, sir." Jacob tried to ignore the word *yet* as he tossed his empty popcorn bag into a nearby trash can. Was his mission truly that impossible? "She's been busy this morning. We haven't had a chance to talk." Unless she'd been avoiding him, which if that were the case, he couldn't blame her. But he had to try.

The chief's brow furrowed with concern. "I don't think putting it off will help your cause any."

"I was actually trying to find her when I ran into you." Jacob looked around and shrugged. "But I think there are over a hundred people here now. I can't find her."

The chief snorted. "You just haven't tried hard enough." He straightened to his full height, his uniform looser across his chest now than before. He cupped his hands around his mouth and boomed, "Has anyone seen Marissa Hawthorne?"

A dozen arms pointed toward the road, and the chief beamed as he clapped Jacob on the shoulder. "I expect a full report in one hour."

The chief hobbled away with Marissa's mother pressed close to his side, leaving Jacob in a confusing pile of embarrassment and awe. He should've thought of that sooner, though he doubted his uniform and voice carried anywhere near the authority of the chief's. Jacob made his way toward the road, where the chalk boxes lined the pavement in multiple squares. Stars, hearts, flowers and a variety of other childish pictures squinted at him from the hot pavement. Shading his eyes from the sun, he scanned the area for Marissa. No luck. She must have already left. Maybe he'd head toward the Porta Potties.

Turning, Jacob couldn't help but smile at a picture of a fire truck. Then he did a double take. Beside the truck stood a picture of a stick woman, a stick man and a little stick boy wearing a fireman's hat. His heart skipped and he leaned closer to examine the drawing. It could have been done by anyone, representing any number of families here today. It was the Fireman's Festival, after all. But he searched the drawing harder, desperate to find any clue that would give merit to the hope now rising in his chest and threatening to cut off his circulation.

There. Sudden joy pierced his lungs and Jacob exhaled sharply. In the bottom left corner were scrawled initials.

O.H.

Marissa stood by the face painting tables once again, watching as Owen remained shockingly still for the college student hovering over his cheek with a brush. She had yet to find Jacob to show him their square, but Owen insisted he couldn't wait another minute to get his face done. She'd have to keep searching for Jacob when Owen was through. Jittery nerves clawed her senses and she shifted her weight, ready to find Jacob and see his reaction before she could dare to hope any further. The future had never been so uncertain, yet she had to stand here beside a bright palette of colors as if everything were normal.

With red paint, the teen carefully began the outline of a fire truck. For the first time, the sight brought more joy than pain, and Marissa drew a deep breath of relief. *Thank You, Lord.* She could do this, with God's help. One fire truck at a time.

"Marissa!"

She heard Jacob's voice before she saw him, his tone loud and slightly panicked. She turned and searched the crowd, finally spotting him jogging toward her. His wide smile disarmed the panic rising in her chest, and she clutched her heart as he came to a stop beside her. "You nearly scared me to death. Why all the yelling?" His grin was contagious, and she didn't hesitate as he took her hand, threading his fingers through hers.

"I've been trying to find you." His breathing slowed to a more regular pace and he shuffled a step closer. "I've looked everywhere."

"So have I." Marissa gulped at the emotion darkening his eyes and tried to decipher it. Hope. Fear. She could relate.

"I saw the chalk box."

She licked her lips, anxiety cutting off all the words she'd planned to say.

He brushed his fingertips along the side of her cheek, and she shivered despite the noon sun shining down on them both. "Does it mean what I hope it means?"

Marissa nodded, catching his hand with her free

one and clutching it close. "I realized something after leaving the hospital." Tears burned the back of her throat, and she struggled to continue. "I've been so foolish. So afraid."

Jacob tightened his grip on her hands, urging her to continue.

"But I don't want to be scared anymore. It's not about avoiding risks, but loving through them. Trusting through them." She drew courage from Jacob's strength and stared straight into his eyes, forgetting the fact that she was opening her heart before the entire community and her own son. "I'm choosing life. Choosing you." She smiled as a rogue tear slipped down her cheek. "That is, if you'll still have me."

Jacob caught the tear with his finger and wiped it on his jeans. "That's the craziest thing I've ever heard. Of course I'll still have you."

"We can talk to my dad together," Marissa rushed, not wanting Jacob to yank back to reality as she'd done too many times before. "We can convince him, I'm sure of it. In fact, he's supposed to be here today. Maybe we can—"

Jacob's finger, still damp with her tears, pressed gently against her lips. "I've already handled it."

Her eyes widened. "You talked to my dad? When?"

"After you left me in the hospital."

He'd pursued her, even after her rejection? Respect and love flooded her veins and she stepped closer. "You're my hero, you know that?"

"That's all I want. I love you, Marissa." He leaned forward, drawing her close and resting his forehead against hers. "And because of that, I'm taking a new job at work as a driver."

Marissa jerked back. "Driver? But what about firefighting?"

Jacob explained the rules of his new promotion. "I would still fight some fires, but not as many. I'd be manning the truck on calls." He shrugged. "You and Owen are worth more to me than any job."

"I can't let you change positions because of me." Marissa shook her head, regret squeezing her chest in a vice. It sounded tempting, so very tempting, but she wouldn't let their relationship begin on resentment.

"It's the best thing for my career." Jacob caught her cheek with his hand, stopping her incessant protest. "But more importantly, it's the best thing for us. I figure this is the first of many compromises." He grinned, a teasing gleam lighting his eyes. "For instance, am I going to kiss you three times? Or four?"

Marissa leaned in, matching his smile with her own and nuzzling his cheek. She whispered in his ear, "I'll compromise. What about five?"

His grip on her waist tightened, and he tilted

his head to line up with hers. Marissa closed her eyes and held her breath, anticipating, every fiber of her being on high alert.

"Eww, are you going to kiss?" Owen's high-pitched protest jerked them apart, and Marissa laughed as her son abandoned his chair to stand beside them.

"You sure you know what you're getting into?" Marissa put a steadying hand on Owen's shoulder, refusing to let go of Jacob's hand with the other.

He squeezed it before slowly tugging free. "I know exactly." He squatted down to Owen's level and smiled. "Hey, buddy, if you let me kiss your mom, I'll take you to the jumping booth."

Owen squinted at Jacob as if in deep thought, then nodded. He covered both eyes with his hands. "Hurry up and you've got a deal."

Jacob quickly stood and took Marissa into his arms. "You've heard the man. Make it snappy."

Marissa wrapped her arms around Jacob's neck and kissed him soundly, oblivious to the whistles and catcalls from the crowd that had gathered around them. She didn't care. She was proud of her hero. Her fireman.

Her answer to her prayer.

They broke apart and Owen peeked between his fingers. "Okay, let's go." He reached out for Jacob and prodded him forward.

"We'll be back." Jacob winked at Marissa, then

ruffled the top of Owen's hair as they strolled together toward the inflatable jumping station.

Marissa couldn't help but admire their forms, growing smaller in the crowd as they walked side by side. She could get used to that, and had the feeling such a scene would become quite familiar over time.

Liz rushed up to Marissa, nearly knocking her sideways as she grabbed her into a hug. "I saw the whole thing! I'm so happy I could cry." Liz kept one arm slung around Marissa's shoulder. "I can't believe he kissed you like that and then just left you alone." She playfully bumped her hip into Marissa's to show she was joking.

"Oh, I'm definitely not alone." Marissa smiled as she watched her future eagerly climb inside the giant jumping booth. "I've got my father back, and a fireman and a junior fireman who I know will do their best to stick around a long time." She leaned into Liz's hug. "And a certain stubborn new friend who never gave up on me."

"I'm always right, you know." Liz let out an exaggerated sigh. "I wish Ryan would realize that as easily as you have."

Marissa laughed, enjoying Liz's company as she watched Owen and Jacob play, her heart full to bursting. No, she'd never be alone again. Thanks to Liz and Jacob, she now had access back not only to her earthly dad but also to her Heavenly Father, who promised in His word never to leave her or forsake her.

And that was a promise she could put her trust in.

Epilogue

Six months later

The late November sun streamed through the bridal window of Orchid Hill Church, coaxing dust fairies into a celebratory dance amidst the beams of light. Marissa stood before the full-length mirror, smoothing the front of her fitted white gown. "Do you think I should have gone tea-length? This isn't my first wedding." She frowned at her reflection, nerves skittering through her stomach.

"But it's Jacob's first—and only, I might add." Liz knelt on the floor in her hunter green dress and fluffed the short train of Marissa's gown. "Besides, after all you two have been through, there's no way you're going into this halfheartedly." She struggled to stand in her heels.

"Trust me. It's anything but halfhearted." Marissa studied her reflection, the tiny sequins on the trim of her dress catching the light and twinkling with secret smiles. Marissa smiled back so wide she feared she smudged her lipstick. All doubts about her appearance fled. She was getting married. To Jacob.

In fifteen minutes.

"Mom!" The door to the bridal room burst open, and Owen ran inside, Olivia on his heels, her long green hair ribbons trailing behind. Owen's bow tie was crooked on his tux and he waved what looked like a blown-up photograph at Marissa. "Dad asked me to give you this and I almost forgot!" Panic lit his expression.

It only took a minute for Marissa's brain to convert "Dad" to "Jacob," as Owen had insisted on calling him since their engagement months before. Marissa took the object from her son and went to kiss him before remembering her lipstick. She straightened his tie instead. "You look handsome, buddy." Then she glanced down at the item in her hand, and her breath hitched. It was the photo of their chalk square from the festival six months ago, the marker of the moment where everything had finally come together—on the pavement and in her heart. She'd almost forgotten about it after Jacob told her the photos had been delayed from the photographer. How sneaky.

She studied the stick figures she'd so carefully crafted with Owen, and warmth seeped through her heart. With a smile, she turned the photo over and immediately recognized Jacob's messy scrawl, written in thick black cursive.

This picture was taken on the day I won your heart.
And today, November 19th, is the day I get to keep trying forever.
All my love, Jacob

"Wow, he's more of a romantic than I thought." Liz's sudden voice over Marissa's shoulder stopped the tears welling in Marissa's eyes just before they spilled over. She blinked rapidly in an effort to save her makeup. No kidding. *Lord, I can't believe I ever doubted Your plan for me.*

"Hey, no crying!" Liz fanned her hands in front of Marissa's face. "That's probably why Jacob intended for you to have this earlier than ten minutes before the ceremony." She laughed as Owen shrugged sheepishly. She did a double take. "Olivia, come here, baby. Your ribbon is falling out."

Liz secured her daughter's hair ribbon just as another knock sounded on the door. "Man entering the sacred suite." Chief Brady's booming voice entered before he did. "It's showtime." His tone gentled as his gaze settled on Marissa. "You look beautiful."

"Thanks, Dad. I'm just so glad you're here." Marissa hugged her father, thirty pounds lighter but still the same bear she always knew. Except, these days he was more teddy than grizzly. He hugged her back, then gestured for Liz to take the kids into position. "They're lining up in the hallway."

"You heard the man. Places!" Liz ushered the kids out of the room. She turned and gave Marissa a parting grin. "I don't know if 'break a leg' is proper terminology for a wedding march."

"Let's not risk it." Marissa laughed, dabbing her still-damp eyes with her fingertips. "See you soon—sis." She waved as Liz blew a kiss and disappeared into the foyer.

"This wedding stuff agrees with you." The chief wrapped his arm around Marissa as they took their place beside the double front doors of the church. "You know you're marrying a winner, huh?"

"I know, Dad," Marissa whispered, emotion lodging in her throat. Anticipation rocked her forward on her heels, and she wanted to jump up and down as Owen had the night Jacob proposed using his toy fire truck as the prop for the ring. The memory brought another smile, and the urge to cry finally subsided as unadulterated joy took its place.

The faint strains of "Canon in D" drifted down

the aisle as Liz strolled to her spot on the stairs beside Pastor Rob. Olivia graced the carpeted floor with flower petals on her way to the altar and Owen was right beside her with the ring bearer pillow. Marissa held her breath, grateful he only tripped once. It was almost her turn. In a few minutes, they'd all be a family.

"This is it." Her father offered his arm, and Marissa stepped into full view of the main aisle as their guests stood as one with the crescendo of the bridal march.

Nerves pinched her stomach until she caught a glimpse of Jacob's face, lighting her destination at the end of the aisle like a beacon in the night. His smile mirrored all the happiness she felt inside and reflected it back as she slowly made her way toward him. Gratitude filled her heart at God's goodness, and she wanted to weep again at the thought that her fears had nearly kept her from this moment. Gazing into Jacob's eyes, she'd never felt more like a princess.

Owen bounced on the balls of his feet as Marissa drew near, and the chief quickly handed Marissa off to Jacob. They turned to face the pastor just as Owen couldn't contain his excitement any longer. "I'm getting a dad today, and he's a fireman!" he hollered, and a chuckle rolled through the congregation.

"Come here, buddy." All desire for protocol

fled and Marissa held out her arm for Owen. He easily slipped into place between her and Jacob, beaming. Together, they faced the pastor three-fold, ready for their vows.

Ready to become a family.

* * * * *

Dear Reader,

As authors, we're often instructed to "write what we know." While I thankfully have not had to experience life as a single mom, I have experienced life as a fireman's wife and as an unemployed fireman's wife. If this story was real, I would be Liz. My husband was laid off from our city's fire department in December 2009 because of city budget cuts, just like in the story. He spent two years in service, missing family events and holidays for the job he wanted to make a lifelong career—for what seemed like nothing. My similarities with Liz stop at the circumstances, however, because she easily reached a level of trust in God that took me nearly a year to obtain. I had days of faith, but had more days when I looked at my toddler and simply cried, not understanding why God would have me reach my dream of becoming a stay-at-home mom only to send me straight back to the workforce nine months later. But like Liz realized early on, God is still God regardless of where paychecks come from. He always provides for His children—sometimes through other people, sometimes through the sweat of your brow and sometimes through mysterious envelopes of cash tucked into your child's diaper bag at church. He did all of the above for us during our time of need and He'll do the same for you if you seek Him first. He will never leave you and will not forsake you! Hold tightly to His promises today.

Many blessings,

Betsy St. Amant

Questions for Discussion

1. Motherhood is often a challenge. As a single mom, how did Marissa struggle more so than other mothers?

2. Marissa lost her husband to a dangerous career. How did this shade her view of heroes?

3. Marissa had a bad relationship with her father because of resentment she carried over from childhood. Have you ever let a childhood grudge affect your adult life?

4. Despite her struggles in her first marriage, Marissa made every effort not to speak negatively of her late husband in front of her son. Do you think this was hard to do? Why is it important for her to do so?

5. Because of his father and grandfather, young Owen also wanted to become a fireman. Why do you think this panicked Marissa?

6. Why did Marissa think Jacob would become a bad influence on her son?

7. In the story, the community banded together to help raise money for the families of those

laid off from the fire department. Has your city ever done something like that to help others? Did you contribute? Why or why not?

8. Marissa found herself drawn to Jacob even though she feared a future with him because of his career. Have you ever been attracted to someone you didn't think you should get involved with? How did you handle it?

9. Liz became a good friend to Marissa as they worked together on the festival. How did Liz help lead Marissa back to the Lord? Has a friend ever helped you in such a way?

10. Marissa, while once close to God, grew distant after the tragedy she endured. Why do you think Christians sometimes pull away from God in the midst of their personal storm instead of drawing closer?

11. The chief's health scare encouraged Marissa to let go of the past and opened her eyes to the possibilities of the future. Has a near tragedy or incident ever done the same for you? How did you respond?

12. Marissa's job was a professional party/event planner. What would be your favorite part of that job? What would be your least favorite part?

13. Jacob feared his interest in the chief's daughter would endanger his position in the department, especially after the recent layoffs that affected his younger brother. Do you think the chief would be right or wrong in targeting Jacob for his feelings for Marissa?

14. As an older brother, Jacob felt responsible for Ryan and his family after the layoff. Have you ever been in the position to help a family member in need? What happened?

15. Despite being rejected multiple times, Jacob never gave up on pursuing Marissa's heart. Have you been in a similar situation with your spouse or significant other? Do you find the notion romantic?

LARGER-PRINT BOOKS!

GET 2 FREE
LARGER-PRINT NOVELS
PLUS 2 FREE
MYSTERY GIFTS

Love Inspired®

SUSPENSE
RIVETING INSPIRATIONAL ROMANCE

Larger-print novels are now available...

LARGER-PRINT BOOKS!

**GET 2 FREE
LARGER-PRINT NOVELS
PLUS 2 FREE
MYSTERY GIFTS**

Larger-print novels are now available...